D0711081

The COLOR *of a*
PROMISE

Julianne MacLean

The Color of a Promise
Copyright © 2016 Julianne MacLean

All rights reserved.

ISBN-13: 978-1-927675-36-6

Cover Design: The Killion Group, Inc.
Interior Formatting: Author E.M.S.

PART I

Prologue

Jack Peterson

It's kind of embarrassing to come back from the dead and still not *get it*. One would think, after something as profound as a close brush with death, you would have a greater understanding of your true purpose and how to steer your life in the right direction. I regret to say that's not what happened to me. It wasn't until much later—years in fact—that I realized the significance of certain events in my life. Before then, I thought I knew everything. In actuality, I had been living in the dark.

Now I see how arrogant I was, believing things were a certain way, and that my life was more extraordinary than others'.

I suppose, in my defense, there *was* something special about me. Something I kept secret because few people would ever believe what I knew about life. Most people would call me crazy. Professionally, I couldn't afford to risk being judged or misunderstood because I was ambitious in my career as a television journalist and foreign correspondent for CNN. For appearances sake, I had to keep quiet about my personal beliefs if I wanted to remain in Afghanistan, covering the war.

But there was, of course, more to my desire to remain in Afghanistan than just my career as a journalist. There was a reason I hadn't wanted to return to the United States. At first, I thought it was heartbreak that kept me away—because I had been jilted by the woman I'd believed to be "the one."

Later, I came to realize it had more to do with my ego, because I had lost that woman to my brother Aaron, who had always been my rival. He had been the one to win her heart, and for a long time, I was angry about that and chose to break away from my family.

Now I understand the truth. I know that what kept me away was not bitterness toward my brother, nor was it my bruised ego. It was fate—because the timing hadn't been right. The moment had not yet arrived to fulfill a promise I had made many years earlier.

CHAPTER

One

I don't think anyone can deny that staring death in the
eye is a wakeup call. The woman I fancied myself in love
with—the one who had jilted me for my brother—had
spoken to me about that once. Her name was Katelyn, and
she had been involved in a cycling accident where she flew
over the handlebars of her bicycle and nearly tumbled over
the edge of a steep cliff. By some miracle, she had lived to
tell the tale.

When she described it to me, she explained that in that
instant, her life had flashed before her eyes with astounding
clarity. A common occurrence for many people.

Or so I've heard.

In my case, there was no time for reflection in the
flashing, terrifying instant of my impending doom. All I
recall is the thunderous sound of the bomb going off, and
an explosion of dust outside the car windows, followed by a
violent jolt as our vehicle flipped over half a dozen times
before bursting into flames.

I wish I could report that while I was clinically dead for approximately ninety seconds in the helicopter while the doctor performed CPR on me, my experience was magical and awe-inspiring and provided irrefutable evidence about the existence of heaven.

The reality is this: I have no memory of angels singing, neither do I recall floating out of my body to watch from above while I was brought back to life. I remember nothing about being pulled from the burning wreck by a team of American soldiers who had been following close behind us on the road. Nor do I remember anything about the trip to the hospital. I don't know where my mind went during all of that, for I recall nothing but blackness, until the moment I regained consciousness in Germany.

That is not to say that I didn't reflect upon my life when I woke. I thought about it a great deal after I opened my eyes and discovered that the person at my bedside—the first of my family members to arrive in Germany—was the last person on earth I wanted to see.

CHAPTER

Two

My older brother Aaron was one of those exceptional individuals who seemed to be born under a shining star. Between the two of us, he had always been the better-looking one. He got straight A's without breaking a sweat, while I was a consistent B student and had to work hard for my grades. While Aaron was captain of the basketball team and went on to become valedictorian of his graduating class, I led a quieter existence as a member of the debating club, where there were no pretty cheerleaders to help us celebrate our wins or take the sting off our losses.

It was obvious to everyone that Aaron was athletic and popular, while I was more of a silent, brooding intellectual who, as a quintessential "angry young man," read *Newsweek* and *The Economist*, and studied the classics and political science in college. Aaron, meanwhile, was making a name for himself in the sailing community—buying old boats, refurbishing them and racing them for medals that gained him a reputation that would later pay off in spades. Aaron had always belonged with the elite.

And yes, I will be the first to admit that part of our rivalry stemmed from jealousy on my part, but not because he was better looking or more popular—and later, far wealthier than me.

The fact of the matter was this: Our rivalry began eons before all that, with extremely deep roots in the past. But I won't go back quite that far at the moment, because that's a story for another day. As far as today is concerned, *this* is what you need to know about Aaron and me. It's the thing that truly matters, although I had no notion of its importance while it was happening.

Chicago 1984

"This is definitely true love," I said to my friend Gordon during lunch hour, as we sat down on the bench by the chain-link fence. We each withdrew a sandwich from our lunch bags.

We were thirteen years old. This was seventh grade.

We both sat transfixed as Jeannie Morrison pulled a comb from the back pocket of her designer jeans and ran it through her long, gleaming, jet-black hair. She laughed at something one of her friends said, and I marveled at her perfect, straight white teeth and full lips, and how glamorous she was. Then the girls all turned to look over their shoulders at the grade nine boys playing soccer on the field.

Jeannie flipped her hair, and as she was sliding the comb back into her pocket, she glanced in my direction. Our eyes locked and held from opposite sides of the basketball court, and my heart began to race as she stared at me for a long moment. I swear on my life, I stopped breathing and all the blood raced to a halt in my veins. Then Jeannie lowered her gaze shyly and glanced up at me again with a coy expression, before she winked.

It was one of those unforgettable, life-changing experiences I knew I would replay in my mind for years to come. I couldn't believe she had looked at me that way. I'd always thought she was the most beautiful girl on the planet, ever since she moved into the big house at the bottom of our street four years earlier. We didn't hang out or anything. I never had the courage to talk to her. But it appeared that *finally* my time had come, probably because I had grown three inches over the summer.

I decided right then and there that it was time to grow up, because Jeannie Morrison was in the eighth grade. She needed a *man*.

Gordon whistled. "*Holy cow patty*," he said with amazement. "Did you see the way she just looked at you?"

"Of course I saw it," I replied, "but don't make a big deal out of it. Just eat your sandwich and act cool." My heart pounded for the rest of the lunch hour while I stole glances at her whenever I could, and hoped for a repeat of that exhilarating wink.

She did look at me again—only once—but I quickly looked away. She did the same.

Later, when the bell rang and everyone filed through the double doors for afternoon classes, Jeannie and I bumped elbows.

"Hey, Jack," she said with a flirty grin. "I like your shirt."

"Thanks," I replied, making an effort to sound laid back. "I like yours too."

She smiled again and nudged me hard with her elbow,

knocking me a few steps to the left. I shoved her back and she laughed. Then we went our separate ways down the wide hall, past all the lockers to our respective home rooms.

I went to sleep that night feeling as if I were floating…miles and miles above cloud nine.

The following day during lunch hour, I sat down with Gordon on our usual bench by the chain-link fence inside the basketball court.

Normally I was a decent student, but I hadn't paid much attention in class that morning. This was out of character for me, but I didn't care. All that mattered was the spectacular possibility that Jeannie Morrison might talk to me again—or even *look* at me—during lunch break. If she did, it would be enough excitement to fuel my happiness for an entire year and thrust me like a bullet out of bed each morning to arrive at school on time.

Sure enough, not long after Gordon and I finished our sandwiches, she came walking over…along the center line of the basketball court with her four friends close behind. I nearly choked on the last bite of my sandwich as I stuffed the crusts into the cellophane wrap and shoved it into the paper bag. Then I balled that up and shoved everything into my backpack.

"Crap, she's coming over here," Gordon said, sitting up straighter.

"I know. Just act cool," I quickly replied.

"Hey guys," Jeannie said with a smile. "What's going on?"

"Not much," I replied with a shrug.

She sat down beside me, while one of the girls from seventh grade sat next to Gordon. I was pretty sure he must be wetting his pants by then.

The other three girls stood in front of us, chewing gum and blowing bubbles.

"Jack," Jeannie said, nudging me smoothly. "I wonder if you could do a favor for us."

I looked up at the three girls who stood before me and had no idea what to expect. "Sure. What is it?"

Jeannie leaned forward to look at her friend—the one sitting on the bench next to Gordon. "Go ahead, give it to him," she said.

The other girl handed me a letter in a sealed envelope. I took hold of it and turned it over. There was nothing written on it.

"This is Millicent," Jeannie said. "She just moved here from Arizona."

Gordon and I both turned to her. "Hi."

"Hi," she said, blushing.

I turned back to Jeannie. "What's this for?"

Jeannie leaned closer and whispered in my ear, as if she were about to tell me an important secret. "Millicent has a thing for your brother. Will you give him that letter?"

Ah. So it wasn't really *me* she had come to see. As always, it was Aaron they were after.

I turned on the bench to glance over my shoulder to where my brother was kicking a soccer ball around on the field with the other grade nine boys.

"Sure," I replied as I slid it into the backpack at my feet. "I'll give it to him tonight."

The three girls in front of us giggled and whispered to each other excitedly, then urged Millicent up off the bench and dragged her off to giggle some more on the other side of the court.

Jeannie sat for a moment, watching them. I didn't know what to say. I had a lump of disappointment in my gut the size of a watermelon.

Then she stood up.

"For the record," she said, sliding her hands into the front pockets of her jeans, "Millicent's the one who likes your brother. Not me."

I had to squint to look up at her because the blinding sun was directly behind her head. "That's cool," I replied.

She hesitated. "I'll see you later, Jack."

With my stomach doing flip flops, I watched her walk away and rejoin her friends.

"Did you hear what she just said?" Gordon asked. "She practically came right out and said that she likes you."

"No, she didn't," I replied, trying to act as if it didn't matter, while my insides were on fire, because I thought maybe…just maybe…it might be true.

"Yeah, she *did*," Gordon argued.

Just then, Jeannie glanced back at me again, and smiled.

Oh, man. I was a goner. "Do you really think—?"

"Yeah, I do," Gordon replied. "You should ask her out."

"I don't know. What if she says no?"

"She won't. She really likes you. Can't you tell?"

Still not ready to believe it and risk rejection by asking out the prettiest girl in the school, I decided to play it cool and wait for more confirmation, in some form or another.

When the bell rang and we all crowded around the doors to go back inside, I received that confirmation. Jeannie nudged her way closer and passed me a note.

I immediately unfolded it. As I read it, I found it difficult to keep my balance going up the steps. It said: *Walk home with me after school?*

All I could do was stop and turn to her. Feeling completely lost in those bewitching blue eyes, I said, "I'll meet you outside when the bell rings."

"Great." She smiled, went inside, and disappeared down the hall.

I don't remember a single thing any of my teachers taught me that afternoon because I was lovesick the rest of the day.

T hank God Aaron and I were no longer confined to the same bedroom. We'd always fought constantly, even as preschoolers, so Mom and Dad eventually separated us and converted the attic into a bedroom for Aaron. Besides being away from me, he preferred it because he could play his music loud and no one would say a word, while Mom was always yelling at me to turn down the volume.

It wasn't often that I ventured up those creaky wooden steps to Aaron's domain. He was surprised to see me after supper that night, with an envelope in my hand.

I didn't enjoy giving it to him. Part of me just wanted to burn it, because the last thing I wanted was to hand him something that would make him even more conceited than he already was—because girls always fell for him and he knew it. I hated to watch it happen, but at least in this case, it wasn't Jeannie who had asked me to deliver a love letter. It was that other girl.

Aaron was seated at his desk doing homework. When he saw me appear at the top of the stairs, he turned in his chair and set down his pencil. "Hey," he said, no doubt surprised to see me.

I flicked the envelope through the air like a paper airplane, because I absolutely refused to deliver it to his desk like a servant. "This is from a girl in seventh grade," I said. "She asked me to give it to you."

I didn't wait for Aaron to open and read it. I just turned around and descended the stairs, went back to my own room and spent the rest of the night dreaming about Jeannie Morrison—and wondering if she might want to walk home with me again the following day.

~ 🖂

My prayers were answered. Jeannie let me walk her home the next day, and every other day that week. Gordon kept asking when I was going to kiss her, but I couldn't imagine how or when I could attempt something like that, having never kissed a girl before.

By the time Friday rolled around, I didn't know how I would survive the entire weekend without seeing her, so I wrestled up the courage to ask if she'd like to go to a movie with me on Saturday night. It was the first time I'd ever asked a girl out on a real date, and I found myself wishing that I'd cleared it with my parents first, to make sure they would let me go, and to ask if they'd drive us.

But my lack of planning didn't matter in the end, because Jeannie made a face. "I wish I could," she said apologetically, "but I'm going to Mark Hennigar's party. Are you going?"

Struggling to scrape my dignity off the sidewalk, I shrugged indifferently. "I'm not invited."

Her face lit up and she spoke with enthusiasm. "I'm inviting you right now. You should come!"

I felt awkward about it because Mark Hennigar was in the eighth grade. He was into sports like hockey and football. I didn't know him at all and I suspected there wouldn't be too many friends of mine at the party.

"You could bring Gordon," Jeannie said. "Mark won't mind. I'll tell him you're both coming with me."

Still feeling weird about it, I said, "What about your friends…Kimmy and Natalie and that new girl?"

"They're all coming, too," Jeannie said. "See? Everyone's going to be there."

We started walking again, but I still felt unsure. "I don't know."

"Please, Jack? It won't be the same if you aren't there. I won't have any fun."

Then it happened. She touched my arm, gave it a squeeze, and it sent an electric jolt of exhilaration through my whole body.

"Come on," she said, bumping me with her shoulder. "Say you'll come. I really want to slow dance with you."

Slow dance?

And that was that. My heart was on the ground. I was in a daze.

"Okay," I heard myself saying. "What time are you going?"

"Kimmy's parents are dropping us off at eight." She began to back away as she strolled into her driveway, clutching her books to her chest in the most charming way imaginable. "So I'll see you tomorrow night?" she said hopefully with a delicate raised eyebrow.

"Yeah, I'll see you then."

"Awesome."

I turned to walk up the hill to my house at the top of

the street, resisting the urge to take off in a run, because I wasn't sure if she might still be watching me through her front window. As always, I wanted to play it cool.

~*~

"You should totally kiss her tonight," Gordon said as we walked through the dark neighborhood toward Mark Hennigar's house, a few blocks away from where I lived.

"I don't want to rush it," I said. "If it happens, it happens."

"Don't be a chicken. My mom always says that you don't get anywhere in life by waiting for stuff to happen. You have to go out there and grab what you want."

I shook my head at the ground. "I doubt she was talking about me kissing Jeannie Morrison for the first time. I'm definitely not going to 'grab' her."

Gordon continued to try and persuade me. "Mom was talking about *everything*. Besides, if you don't kiss Jeannie, she'll think you're not interested. And remember, she's in the eighth grade. She's used to older guys who know what they're doing. She's going to expect more from you than a peck on the cheek."

I doubted most of the guys in the eighth grade knew what they were doing any more than I did, but Gordon did have a point. I didn't want Jeannie to think I wasn't interested, but I had no idea how to get further than a peck on the cheek. It made my stomach roll with nervous knots.

When we rang the doorbell, Mark's dad greeted us at the door, told us to keep our shoes on, and sent us downstairs to the rec room—a wide open space, completely dark except for a few strings of colored Christmas lights draped from the ceiling. A long table with a plastic checkered tablecloth stood against the wall with bowls full of chips and cheese sticks. Beneath it, there was a cooler on the floor, filled with ice and canned pop. Bon Jovi's *Wanted Dead or Alive* was blasting from a stereo in the corner, and though it was precisely 8:00 p.m., we realized we were early. There were only three girls in the room, seated on the brown sofa. We had no idea who they were, and we were too shy to go and talk to them.

"Let's get something to drink," Gordon said as we moved across the room to the snack table. We busied ourselves with cheese sticks and cola, and looked up uneasily when Mark Hennigar came bounding heavily down the stairs with about six guys.

To our immense relief, he gave us a nod and said, "Hey guys," before he leaped onto the sofa next to the girls and made them laugh and squeal.

The other guys went to change the music, and I felt about as comfortable as a zebra in a raincoat.

Then the doorbell rang. I heard the sound of laughter and conversation upstairs. About thirty seconds later, the basement was full of kids—but still, we didn't know anyone very well.

I never felt so uncomfortable in my life. I just wanted to sink through the floor and crawl home. Gordon looked pale and fidgety.

Then the doorbell rang again.

I watched the stairs expectantly.

My heart dropped.

There she was. *At last.*

Jeannie and her friends came hurrying down. She paused on the bottom step, scanned the dimly lit room for a moment, and found me. Our eyes met and her face lit up with a smile. She waved at me, and suddenly I had no desire to leave the party. Somehow I knew I was exactly where I was meant to be.

Looking back on it now, I recognize how true that sentiment was—even though the night turned out to be as disastrous as any night can be when you're thirteen years old, and head over heels in love with the prettiest girl in school.

CHAPTER

Five

Shortly before 10:00 p.m., a bunch of kids went outside to sit on white plastic lawn chairs arranged in a circle on the grass, even though it was the middle of October and too cold to be sitting outside without a jacket.

The cold didn't bother *me* of course. How could it, when I was feeling on top of the world—because five minutes earlier, Jeannie and I had slow danced in the dark, and I was brave enough to kiss her—to make out with her, actually—to the tune of Lionel Richie's *Hello*.

Afterward, Gordon questioned me insistently about what it was like, but I didn't want to talk about the particulars. It was private, between me and Jeannie. She and I were an item now, and I was already planning when and how I would ask her to junior prom, which was still an entire school year away.

Gordon and I sat down on a couple of chairs under the deck because we didn't know anyone on the grass. I checked my watch. My parents expected us home by 11:00, and it was almost 10:30.

Then the most unexpected thing happened. That new girl, Millicent, spotted us and approached, stomping up the grass as if she were on a mission. Gordon sucked in a breath, and I wondered if he might have a thing for her, because she was kind of cute. Not beautiful like Jeannie, but there was something awkward and nerdy about her, which Gordon probably found attractive.

"Hi Jack," she said, standing in front of us.

"Hi Millicent," I replied.

She shifted uneasily and looked around. "Are you having fun?"

"Yeah, it's an okay party," I replied, even though on the inside, I was bouncing up and down on a mental pogo stick.

Her shoulders rose and fell with a frustrated sigh and she looked me straight in the eye, accusingly. "Did you give my letter to your brother?"

Here we go...

"Yes."

"Did he read it?"

"I don't know. I think so."

She blew out another quick breath, as if she were frustrated with me. "He was supposed to be here tonight. Do you know if he's coming?"

I shrugged again. "He didn't mention anything, but we don't talk much."

Just then, the sliding glass doors opened and three of Aaron's friends walked out. Millicent gasped and watched them stroll onto the grass and join the others.

"He's here," she whispered, watching the door and waiting for him to step out as well, but he didn't. Her eyebrows pulled together in a frown. "Where is he?"

She sat down between Gordon and me. "What should I do? He's probably inside. Should I go in? Should I try and talk to him?"

"Wow, you've got it bad," Gordon said.

"I can't help it," she replied, sounding all swoony and in love. "He's just so cute."

Cute? She thought Aaron was *cute?*

She took hold of my arm and shook me. "I need to do something, Jack, or I'll go crazy. Will you come inside and introduce me to him? Even if he read the letter, I'm not sure he even knows who I am."

My head drew back in surprise. "You've never talked to him before?"

"No, he's in the ninth grade!" As if that explained everything.

"Did you sign your name to the letter or was it anonymous?" Gordon asked.

"I signed my name," she replied. "And I caught him looking at me yesterday at recess, but I don't know how he feels. Could you ask him?"

"*Me?*" Was she nuts?

"You're his brother."

"Just because we're brothers doesn't mean we like each other." I paused. "What does Jeannie say? You should ask *her.*"

Millicent huffed. "Jeannie was the one who encouraged me to write the letter in the first place and tell him how I felt, but it's not working. I wish he would just talk to me. Or *something.*"

"Maybe he's just not interested," Gordon said, and I gave him a look, because Millicent didn't seem in any state to hear something like that. The poor girl was obsessed.

"Please, Jack?" she asked. "Will you come inside and help me talk to him?"

Though it was the last thing on earth I wanted to do, I

said yes because Jeannie was in there, and I figured I could use the excuse to ask her to dance with me again. So I got up and went inside with Millicent.

~*O*

"Where is he?" Millicent asked, looking around the dark rec room where a few kids were slow dancing to *Against All Odds*.

I led her to the snack table, which had been replenished in the last half hour. "Look, they have Doritos."

I grabbed a handful and stuffed them into my face, then glanced around for Jeannie, but I didn't see her either.

"Did he not come?" Millicent asked, growing increasingly frustrated. She boldly walked up to Kimmy, who was waltzing with some guy. Millicent tugged at her arm. "Did you see Aaron come in?"

Kimmy stared at her for a few seconds and glanced around awkwardly. "I don't know."

"His friends came in a few minutes ago," Millicent told her. "Was he with them?"

The guy waltzing with Kimmy leaned closer to speak loudly over the music. "He's in the closet with Jeannie."

Millicent and I both responded at the same time. "*What?*"

I felt stunned and paralyzed, while steam came out of Millicent's ears. She marched straight over to the closet, flicked on the overhead lights, and whipped the door open.

There they were, for all the world to see, lips smacking and hands groping.

They jumped apart at the intrusion, and everyone in the rec room shouted at Millicent to turn off the lights, but she simply stood there, motionless, staring. I did the same from across the room, unable to swallow the Doritos in my mouth.

"You were supposed to be my friend," she said to Jeannie. "You said we were blood sisters!" Then she turned and ran up the stairs.

Some other kid moved to switch off the lights, while Jeannie reached out to shut the closet door again. She met my gaze for a second, and simply shrugged with what struck me as an apology—as if to say: *What did you expect? It couldn't be helped.*

My stomach dropped, and I wanted to pound my brother into the ground. But he was bigger than me and I knew I'd end up getting pounded—in front of everyone.

So I went outside to get Gordon and we left in a hurry, up the stairs and out the front door. It wasn't easy to pass by the closet a second time, knowing the great love of my life was in there necking with the brother I despised. I wanted to cry, but not in front of everyone. Another part of me just wanted to hit something.

Outside, we found Millicent, sitting on the curb in tears.

"Hey Millicent," I said gently. We sat down on either side of her. "Are you okay?"

She wiped tears from her cheeks with the back of her sleeve. "I can't believe she did that."

"Me neither," I replied.

"She's the one who kept telling me to go after him. She'd say things like: 'He's looking at you. I think he likes you. He's checking you out.' But none of it was true, and I don't know why she did that when she liked him all along."

"We thought she liked Jack," Gordon said, and I felt like a fool.

Millicent turned to me. "I know, right? She was walking home with you every day. Did she ever let on that she liked Aaron?"

"Not once," I replied, thinking back on all our conversations, and fighting to keep the hurt inside.

"Some friend she was," Millicent said, shaking her head as a car pulled up. "Here come my parents. I gotta go. See you guys."

We all stood up and backed away from the curb. Millicent got into the car and it drove away, while Gordon and I began to walk home in silence.

After a long while, he said, "You're better off without her."

I shoved my hands into my pockets and shivered in the late October chill. "I guess so. I just thought she really liked me—but I won't be so gullible next time. I think I'll stay away from girls for a while."

I didn't speak to Aaron when he arrived home an hour later, but that was nothing new. When it came to women, I'd learned a long time ago that he would always have the advantage, and he would always win.

What I *didn't* know was that sometimes in life, second place can turn out to be even better than first, for a variety of reasons.

In any case, the race wasn't over yet.

If I thought *I* had it rough on Monday morning—having to face Jeannie with no idea what to say to her—it was ten times worse for Millicent. Not only had she been rejected by the boy she liked, but she had also been betrayed by the girls who had taken her under their wing on her first day at a new school.

At lunch time, Millicent chose not to sit with them, and because she was new in town, she didn't have any other friends to fall back on. Needless to say, I felt as if we had been shot by the same gun, and I sympathized. At least I had my best friend Gordon at my side.

"Look at her," I said to him as we sat on our usual bench in the basketball court, unwrapping our sandwiches. "She's sitting all by herself."

I glanced across at Jeannie and her sickeningly fashionable entourage. They were watching Millicent and giggling.

"Why do they have to be so mean?" I asked. "They're the ones who treated her bad. Now they're making fun of her."

Suddenly, my devastating heartbreak over Jeannie—which had kept me in my room sulking all weekend—turned to rage, and before I had a chance to think about what I was doing, I set down my sandwich and walked straight over to where Millicent was sitting, eating her lunch alone.

I sat down beside her. "Hey. Do you want to come and eat lunch with me and Gordon?"

She barely looked up. "Sure."

Gathering up her sandwich, she stood and crossed the basketball court with me. I couldn't help but glance back at Jeannie and the other girls who were watching us with frowns on their faces.

They turned away after that, left the basketball court, and stopped giggling at Millicent.

~   ◯

After that day, Gordon and I expanded our twosome to a threesome, and Millicent ate lunch with us every day for the rest of the school year. She also came over to my house or Gordon's house on weekends to play *Space Invaders* and *Pacman* and watch movies with us, and she fit in with the two of us as if she weren't a girl at all. We didn't think of her that way because she wasn't beautiful like Jeannie, and she had no interest in either of us, romantically. After the demoralizing debacle at Mark Hennigar's party, I think we were all a little gun shy.

For a time, we commiserated about Jeannie and Aaron, but soon we began to discover that we had a lot more in common than just that. Eventually, we forgot about our broken hearts and all those stupid, mean, giggling girls. We just hung out together and had fun.

From that moment on, my whole world seemed to expand and become new and interesting, because Millicent was really smart and she talked about interesting things—things Gordon and I had never thought about before. Not just girl stuff, either. She knew things about new technology and medicine because her father was a doctor, and she had a room full of tiny dollhouses she had built. They were detailed and intricate, and she told us she wanted to be an architect when she grew up. She also built model cars and airplanes, and Gordon and I soon started building models, too. Not dollhouses, though. We built space ships.

I felt lucky to have the two best friends anyone could ever ask for. I only wish it could have lasted longer than it did.

～⊘

When summer vacation began after seventh grade, the situation improved in the Peterson household. Normally, we all traveled as a family to our summer house on the coast of Maine, but during that particular summer, my mom got a new job with the city and didn't want to ask for time off. So Dad took Aaron to Maine to go fishing and sailing without us, which was fine by me, since it was never my first choice to be stuck on a sailboat with my brother.

As a result, it came as no surprise that, with Aaron gone and my mother working full time, it was the best summer of my life. I had more freedom to go places and do things, without having to constantly check in at home.

Gordon and I spent a lot of time at Millicent's house, because both her parents worked as well, and she had a pool and giant backyard with a small forest beyond the fence. If we weren't swimming in her pool on sunny days, we were biking to the corner store for candy, or venturing into the woods to catch fish with our hands in the river, or making plans to build a fort.

"Why do we have to call it a fort?" Millicent asked. "Let's call it a clubhouse."

"That's such a girlie thing to call it," Gordon argued. "I suppose you'll want to hang curtains and have a tea set."

"Maybe," she replied, defiantly.

I strode past them to walk ahead, searching for a good spot to build our future clubhouse.

"What about right here? The ground is flat and there are four trees in a square. It would be easy to hammer the planks onto the trunks. See what I mean?" I spread my arms wide between two of the trees.

Gordon strode closer. "Except that on a windy day, if the trees sway, the walls will move and it'll probably fall apart."

Millicent came to stand in the center of the square. "The trunks don't move in the wind, not this close to the ground. It's only the treetops that blow around. And these are good and solid." She pounded the edge of her fist on the thick bark. "I think it's a great spot."

"Where will we get the wood?" Gordon asked.

"I can talk to my dad tonight," Millicent replied. "He might agree to buy us some. And he's got everything in his toolshed—hammers and nails and a saw."

"You're going to tell him about this?" Gordon asked, sounding concerned. "What if he says we're not allowed? Because this isn't our land. It's public property. And it's supposed to be a *secret* hideout. If your dad knows about it, it's not a secret anymore. And parents… They just don't get this stuff. They always say no."

"Maybe your parents do, but mine always say yes to

anything that doesn't involve the TV, and they know I want to be an architect someday and design houses, so they'll totally let me do this. Besides, do you have any other ideas about how we can get wood?" Millicent asked.

Gordon looked around. "We could chop down some trees like the pioneers did. Build it like a log cabin."

"Clear-cut this forest?" Millicent replied with horror. "No way! Besides, we'd probably get in trouble for that. There's gotta be a law that says you can't do that, and I'm not breaking the law. Rules are in place for a reason."

I held up a hand. "I vote that we let Millicent ask her dad, because we're going to need tools. There's no way we can keep this a secret if we're going to do it right—and I think we should do it right."

"I agree," Millicent said. "Do you guys want to come for supper tonight? Mom's making spaghetti. We can ask then."

"Sure," I replied.

"I can't," Gordon said. "I have soccer practice."

Millicent turned to me. "Do you still want to come?"

I quickly thought about it. "Yeah."

"Good. Let's head back. It's almost five."

We trudged out of the woods together.

~ 🦋

"So where, exactly, is the spot you picked out?" Millicent's father asked from the head of the table, as soon as he finished saying Grace. We all picked up our forks and dug into our meals.

"It's through the back gate," Millicent explained, "just past the creek. We moved some rocks to make a bridge to get there."

"That was industrious," Dr. Davenport replied, sounding impressed. He turned to look at me and nodded. "Well done."

Millicent's father was a G.P., and I admired him more than anyone I'd ever met. He was smart about everything, and not just doctor stuff. He knew about carpentry and car motors, and he was always talking to us about what was happening in the world—like wars in other countries, or interesting facts about history and politics. He didn't talk down to me, and that's what made me enjoy spending time at the Davenports' house. It's probably also what sparked my early interest in global news and current events, and eventually led me to a career in journalism.

On top of all that, he and Mrs. Davenport were super chill. They laughed about things my uptight parents would have scolded me for. It was a wonderfully relaxed household, not to mention the fact that Millicent and her younger sister Leah were close. There was no conflict or tension around the dinner table because they got along so well. Not like Aaron and me.

Millicent also had an eleven-month-old baby sister named Nina who sat at the table in a high chair and ate chopped up spaghetti with her hands. No one seemed to mind the mess she made.

"How about we all take a walk over there after supper," Dr. Davenport suggested, "and see what's what? There are some logistics to consider—like how you'll haul the wood and tools out there if you have to get everything over the creek. But it sounds like you've picked a good spot, and where there's a will, there's always a way."

He smiled at me directly and I felt a surge of pride and

inspiration—that we *would* get our clubhouse built over the summer.

After Millicent and I helped Mrs. Davenport tidy up the dishes, we all ventured outside, through the gate, to the woods beyond.

Afterwards, we came back to the house for ice cream. While Millicent and I sat at the kitchen table with her two younger sisters, squeezing the bottle of chocolate sauce over our bowls, Dr. and Mrs. Davenport put on a Barry Manilow album in the living room. Dr. Davenport smiled at Mrs. Davenport, took hold of her hand and pulled her, spinning, toward him. Soon they were waltzing to *Weekend in New England*.

From the kitchen, I watched them discreetly, but with fascination, as they whispered in each other's ears, because my parents were never romantic like that.

It was one of those strange, magical moments I knew I'd never forget.

"I really like your parents," I said to Millicent a week later as we worked together, hammering wooden planks to the trees to build the first wall. "I love how your dad trusts us to do this on our own. My dad would never lend me his tools and let me come out here, unless he was right beside me, telling me exactly how to do it the whole time, and making sure I didn't hammer a nail through my hand."

Millicent laughed. "Your dad's nice too, though."

"He's okay." He had more in common with Aaron, which was why they were in Maine together and Mom and I were here.

Gordon was also away that weekend for a soccer tournament, so it was just Millicent and me getting started on the clubhouse. With only the two of us, it was no easy task to haul the wood across the creek, but we were a good team.

We would need Gordon to finish the clubhouse, however, because Millicent's dad had only given us enough material to complete one wall. He promised to get more for us if we all worked together over the summer, doing odd jobs around his house.

That week, I mowed his lawn while Millicent used the whipper snipper and Gordon dug up dandelions. The following week, we agreed to babysit her two younger sisters and paint the deck. In return, Dr. Davenport promised to take us back to the lumber store for another load of wood.

I hammered the last nail into the final plank, while Millicent held it in place. Then we stood back and surveyed our work.

"It looks great," she said, resting her hands on her hips. "We did a good job with the level."

We both moved around the trees to stand inside the square, where we tried to imagine how it would look when it was finished.

"Should we build a wooden floor, too?" Millicent asked. "Or just leave it like it is?"

"I don't know," I replied. "Let's see how comfortable it is."

We sat down on the soft forest floor, which was covered in pine needles and tree roots that jutted out of the ground.

"It would probably be okay with four walls and a roof," Millicent said, "but I think a floor would be nicer. We could even bring some chairs out here."

"It would mean another week of chores," I mentioned, "to earn the extra lumber, but that's okay. I don't mind doing stuff for your dad. Although, I don't know about babysitting your little sisters."

She laughed softly. "Don't worry. It'll be fun. We'll play board games after Nina's in her crib for the night."

We both took a moment to look around and imagine our future clubhouse with four walls and a roof. Then we sighed heavily and flopped onto our backs, looking up at the sky beyond the treetops where the wind whispered gently through the leaves.

For a long while, we just lay there, relaxing.

"I love it here," I said. "This has been the best summer ever."

There was something about Millicent that I found both thrilling and contagious. It was her determination and drive to accomplish something and get what she wanted. I'd seen it in those first few days when she thought she was in love with my brother. She had a single-minded focus that I found annoying at the time. Gordon had called it an obsession, but now I understood, it was just her personality. She was intense about everything, but I liked that about her.

I supposed that was why her parents kept her busy with projects like model airplanes and clubhouses in the woods.

"I really like your family," I said.

"They like you, too." She turned her head to look at me. "Jack, will you promise me something?"

I met her gaze. "Sure."

"Will you promise that we'll always be friends? And that we'll finish this clubhouse together, and that it will always be ours? You, me, and Gordon?"

"I promise," I said.

She let out a contented sigh and looked up at the trees again.

"Can I ask you something else?" she said, after a time. "Something personal?"

"Sure."

She turned her head to look at me again. "Why do you hate your brother so much? I mean…I know you were mad at him for kissing Jeannie, but you say you've never gotten along, not even when you were little. How come?"

I watched the hazy rays of sunlight filter through the green leaves and wondered if I should tell Millicent the truth. As always, something held me back, because it wasn't something I ever talked about. If I did let something slip, people thought I was weird.

She nudged me. "Come on. What is it? You can tell me."

I sat up and looked at her for a moment, considering it. She sat up as well, and for some reason I knew I could trust her, that she would never betray me.

"I don't usually talk about it," I said, "because I *did* talk about it once, and everyone thought I was nuts. Aaron told my mother about the things I was saying, and she took me to the doctor. I ended up having to see a child psychologist and they wanted me to take pills. That's when my mom told them to forget it, and she refused to take me back there, and I learned to keep my mouth shut, and everyone just kind of forgot about it."

"Forgot about what?" Millicent asked, leaning forward slightly with interest. "What happened?"

I took a deep breath, because it was embarrassing. Sometimes I was afraid I was schizophrenic or something, even though I had no idea what that word actually meant.

"When I was little," I explained, "about four or five, I was convinced that I was someone else. That my name was Roger and I was from Canada. I barely remember it, but Mom says I used to insist that she wasn't my real mother."

"Why would you think that?" Millicent asked.

"Because I had memories of another family, and I told her I missed them. She was afraid I was going to say that stuff in public or at school, and people would think I was one of those missing kids, and that she abducted me."

"Do you think…maybe you were?" Millicent asked with wide eyes.

I shook my head and reached for a small twig on the ground, which I twirled around my finger. "No, it was something else. Kind of like another life I had lived before. When I mentioned it again to Aaron a few years later—what I *really* thought was wrong with me—he told me I was crazy and belonged in a mental institution, and that if I told anyone, that's exactly where I'd end up."

"I still don't understand," she persisted. "What did you think was wrong with you?"

I sighed heavily and met her gaze. "Don't laugh, but I think I might be reincarnated, because I remember stuff from other times, too." I tossed the twig away.

She sat back. "Wow. Did you ever see the movie *Audrey Rose*? I watched it last year. It was really creepy. I had nightmares."

"No, I didn't see it," I replied. "What was it about?"

"It's about a girl, our age, who has strange memories and starts acting weird. The same thing happens to her that happened to you. Her parents take her to doctors and psychologists, and finally this man comes and tells them that he thinks the girl is his daughter who died in a car accident, and she's reincarnated. Then he hypnotizes the girl to make her remember. But I won't tell you how it ends."

"Maybe I should watch it," I said.

"Or maybe not," Millicent said. "It's kind of scary."

"I can handle it," I replied.

She hesitated. "Okay. I could ask my parents to rent the video this week. We could make popcorn."

"But don't tell them why," I quickly said. "I don't want them thinking I'm crazy, and I don't want to go back to see any more doctors. Don't even tell Gordon. I don't want anyone to know."

"Just me," she said with a smile.

I gave her a look. "You like knowing secrets, don't you."

"Who doesn't?" she replied.

With that, we rose to our feet and started back to her house.

As we were crossing the creek, she said, "So is that why you don't like Aaron? Because he said you were crazy?"

I stepped gingerly across the rocks and leaped to the other side. "That's part of it," I said. "But I think the real reason is because we were enemies in another time."

She stopped and stared at me. "You think *he's* reincarnated, too?"

I continued walking, and she followed. "I think we *all* are. Most people just don't remember."

CHAPTER

Eight

Germany 2007

"Jack, can you hear me?"

At that point, I had no idea where I was, or how serious my injuries were. All I knew was that I was lying in a hospital bed and I couldn't seem to move my body. In my mind, I felt nothing. It was as if I did not exist in physical form, although I was consciously aware of beeping monitors and the typical antiseptic smells of a hospital.

Somehow I managed to blink repeatedly until my eyelids fluttered open, and my brother's face came into view. He stood over the bed, staring down at me with concern, urging me to speak or do something—*anything*—to indicate that I was conscious and aware of his presence.

"Can you speak, Jack? Are you all right? Can you say something?"

I was confused more than anything, because Aaron's face was not one I expected to see. The last thing I remembered was driving in the Hummer with my cameraman, Paul, and two American soldiers. We were in the middle of a military convoy on our way to a remote location where an entire village had been shaken apart by an earthquake. At that time, my brother Aaron was in America…or so I'd thought. I hadn't seen him or spoken to him in two years. *What was he doing there? And where was I, exactly?* It was all very confusing and unclear.

I made an effort to wet my lips and form words, but my mouth was dry as ash. I swallowed hard, and that was the moment I became aware of the pain. At first it was my head that began to throb, then I felt a deep pounding ache in my right forearm.

Next, the flesh on my abdomen began to burn, as if someone were pouring acid all over me. My breaths came short, and a hot, sudden panic washed over me. I wanted to move, but I couldn't. My heart hammered in my chest and I stared up at Aaron with wide eyes, not knowing what was happening to me.

My God, my leg. It throbbed everywhere—from my pelvis all the way down to the tips of my toes, causing me to scream in agony inside my head.

At last, I managed a word: "*Pain.*"

Aaron nodded and bolted for the door. I heard him shout at someone in the corridor. "He's awake and he's in pain! We need help!"

Nurses and doctors came rushing into the room. The sight of them in such a flurry of activity around my bed only served to increase my anxiety.

"Where am I?" I asked the nurse who was pumping me full of something with a needle in a port. It was attached to a tube that entered my bloodstream, somewhere.

"You're in Landstuhl, Germany," she replied in an

American accent. "We're happy to see you awake, Mr. Peterson. You're a very lucky man."

Lucky?

I'd never known such excruciating pain before, and over the next several hours, as I learned the extent of my injuries, I found myself wishing that I had not woken up at all.

～❂

It wasn't easy for me to comprehend what the doctors were telling me, because I was pumped full of morphine and my brain didn't seem to work very well. But I did my best to make sense of it—that I had been in a coma for the past twenty-four hours and major reconstructive surgery had already been performed on me. They told me I was fortunate because the accident had caused no brain damage or other permanent injuries. Most of the damage was to flesh and bone, which I was told would heal—eventually.

According to the doctor who stood over my bed explaining all of this, my left femur was broken and my knee had been shattered. My face was a bloody, swollen mess from broken glass and flying bits of steel, while my arm was broken in two places. What concerned them most was my torso, which was blistered with third degree burns around my ribcage.

"You'll have a rough road ahead of you," the doctor said. "I won't lie. There's going to be a lot of pain and the rehabilitation will take time, but you *will* walk again Mr. Peterson, and you'll get your life back. You have a lot to be thankful for."

Thankful. The rational part of my brain knew he was right, but I was not concerned with my future in that moment, for nothing seemed the least bit relevant outside the tremendous pain I was in now. Not just the physical pain, but the knowledge that Paul, who had been my closest friend over the past two years, had not survived the accident. Nor had the other two soldiers who were driving in the Hummer with us. I was the only one they had been able to pull from the wreck.

Naturally, I wondered why.

Why me, and not them?

~*

"Why are you here?" I asked Aaron after the doctor left us alone in the private ICU room.

I hadn't meant to be rude, nor was I trying to pick a fight with my brother. I simply found it odd that he, of all people, was the person who had come.

"Mom and Dad are on their way," he explained. "They got on the first flight out of Chicago as soon as they heard, but I was in Amsterdam. I was closest."

My brother owned a successful boatbuilding company based in Maine, with offices and factories all over the world, so he traveled a lot. He was known mostly for his champion racing schooners, and he was a multi-millionaire, married to the woman I had once wanted for myself.

That was Katelyn. The one who had the cycling accident, whose life flashed before her eyes.

"Is Katelyn coming, too?" I asked, hoping the answer would be no, because I didn't want her to see me like this.

I told myself it was not because I was still in love with her. I had worked hard over the past two years to accept that she and Aaron would always be together, and that I had to move on. But she was the reason I had requested this long-term assignment in Afghanistan—because I couldn't bear to watch them together, so unbelievably happy.

I believe Katelyn was well aware of my reason for leaving. Aaron didn't know about this, but when I left the country, she rushed to the airport at the last minute to see me off and hug me tight. She had cried and told me to take care of myself and stay safe. She never wrote to me after that. I believe she knew I needed time and space to forget her and move on.

I imagined she was feeling pretty guilty right now.

"No," Aaron replied. "She can't fly." He gestured with his hands, indicating the size of her belly. "She's due in a month."

I breathed deeply, while my heart thumped heavily in my chest.

"Listen, Jack..." Aaron said, bowing his head and slowly shaking it. "I'm really sorry this happened to you. When I got the call, I was scared you weren't going to make it." His eyes lifted, and in them, I saw a look of regret. A desire to say he was sorry for all the times we fought—both in this life and in others.

Strangely, I felt *nothing* as he spoke. No sudden wish to bury the hatchet. No burning desire to become best friends with him, at long last. As far as I was concerned, nothing had changed. There was simply too much water under the bridge, too many horrendous conflicts in the past that could never be erased. Things I couldn't even speak of now.

"I know we've never been close," Aaron continued, "and we've been at each other's throats for most of our lives, but you're still my baby brother, and I want you to know that I'm here for you...whatever you need. We all want you to come home, Jack. Katelyn wants that, too. You know she thinks the world of you—she always has—and she'd like for our children to know their uncle. I want that, too. If we could just…"

I was afraid he was going to bring up those old conflicts and try again to work things out, but there was no point. There was nothing he could say to make me understand where he was coming from. And hadn't we agreed, years ago, not to talk about it, because it was another life? We were not the same people.

Thankfully, he didn't go there.

"If we could just…*start over*," he said.

Even with the heavy dose of morphine I had been given, the physical pain in every part of my body had not abated, and for that reason, I could not feel sympathy for Aaron's regrets—if that's what they were—nor could I make any decisions about my future. I simply could not think. I was too focused on enduring the throbbing agony in my leg, my arm, and the burns on my left side.

Although…for Aaron to say that we had never been close was the understatement of the century. I closed my eyes, supposing that my accident had been a wakeup call for him, too. It had forced him to consider how fragile life was. Obviously, he wanted to mend what was broken between us. But the last thing I wanted was to return home to the United States in this mangled condition, with a great deal of suffering ahead of me, and have to watch, up close, his perfect life with the woman I had always wanted.

Always.

"I appreciate the sentiment," I said, clenching my teeth and feeling the weight of this conversation take a toll on me, both physically and emotionally, "but I need to rest."

The burns on my side were excruciating, and all the cuts, bruises and swelling on my face made it difficult to speak.

"Of course," Aaron replied, sitting back in his chair. "I'll leave you in peace."

Peace? I wished there could have been peace, but there was only the constant hammering agony in my body and troubling thoughts of my friend Paul and the two American soldiers who had perished, while I, for some reason, had been spared.

I was no stranger to loss, but I wish I had known, in that moment, about the extraordinary events that were looming just over the horizon, and the miracle that was about to touch my life. It might have made the pain of those first few days easier to bear.

CHAPTER

Nine

My parents arrived in Germany that night and came straight to the hospital from the airport. They cried when they walked into the ICU and saw me in bed with my arm in a cast, my leg in traction, and a face looking like someone had taken a sledgehammer to it.

I tried to assure them that I was fine and my wounds would heal. "It's not too painful," I lied.

My mother said, "Your guardian angel must have been watching over you."

My guardian angel... Maybe that was so.

After the initial shock wore off, my parents sat down next to Aaron and began to chat with me about everyday things, obviously trying to cheer me up and make me feel as if my life would soon return to normal. Mom told me about her garden at the summer house in Cape Elizabeth. She said things like, 'Just wait until you see my cucumbers, Jack. You'll be amazed.'

Dad spoke about Great Aunt Norma and her new flame. He was a younger man—only eighty-two. I tried to laugh politely when they called her a cradle robber, but it hurt too much.

Then Mom and Dad fell silent for a few seconds and exchanged a look, as if silently consulting about whether or not they should tell me something in particular.

"What is it?" I asked.

When they continued to hesitate, I said, "Seriously, after what I've been through, I can take anything."

My father inclined his head and raised an eyebrow. "I don't know, Jack. This might freak you out a bit. It's nothing bad…"

I gestured with a hand, and felt very aware of the oxygen monitor clamped to my forefinger, and the tubes dangling everywhere. "You can't say something like that, Dad, and *not* tell me what it is."

My father glanced at my mother for direction, and she merely shrugged, as if to suggest they had no choice but to confess. "He's going to hear about it eventually."

Dad sat forward in his chair, rested his elbows on his knees, and cupped his hands together. "She's right, so we might as well spill the beans."

He glanced at Aaron, who shrugged a shoulder and said, "Go ahead."

Dad looked at me. "All right, Jack. Here it is in a nutshell. At this moment, you're probably the biggest celebrity in the United States of America."

I frowned. "What do you mean?"

Dad struggled to find a way to explain. "Well…you see… The roadside bomb has been the top story on every news station for the past two days. CNN especially, since you're one of their journalists. Everyone's grieving for the soldiers who died, and the whole country has been praying for you to come through. They've been replaying a number of your segments about the war, going over your career.

Remember when you saved that injured woman who was covered in blood? You dropped your microphone and risked your life to carry her away from an explosion. And remember the time you intervened when that young girl was being beaten by her father in the street? How you shouted at her father and you didn't back down? They've been playing all of it, and they've even been talking to people that know you from high school. I don't know how those pictures got out—we certainly didn't share anything—but they have images from that Shakespeare play you were in, where you played Romeo."

"Oh, God." I rolled my eyes. "That was eleventh grade."

"You were so wonderful in that," Mom gushed.

Inside, I didn't know what to make of all this. Whatever was happening in the United States felt like fiction to me. All I knew were the four walls of this hospital room and my constant pain. I could barely respond.

"Jack?" Dad said. "Did you hear what I just said?"

"Yes," I replied. "But I'm sure it'll all blow over when the next big news story hits. That's how it works. They'll forget about me in a few days." And that would be fine with me. I just wanted to be left alone to recover.

Mom, Dad and Aaron shared a look.

"Even if they do move on to another story," Mom said, "isn't it nice to know that so many people are praying for you right now? I wish you could see it, Jack. There's been such an outpouring of love." She pointed at the window. "And the press is here. They're outside the hospital right now, waiting for news about you."

Dad spoke up. "It's all over the Internet. The constant prayers… Millions of people, Jack. It's truly unbelievable.

Would you like us to set up a laptop so you can see what's happening?"

Mom shot him a look and spoke quietly, as if I wouldn't be able to hear her scolding him. "*Stan.* Not yet. I don't want him seeing those images from the bombing. Let's wait until tomorrow."

Part of me didn't want to see them either, but because I was a newsman, I told Dad to open his laptop.

~ *O*

It wasn't easy to look at—the disturbing images of the smashed-up, burned-out Hummer. All I could think about was that three lives had been lost, and the wonder surrounding my survival. How was it even possible? Had I been thrown from the vehicle somehow? How had I escaped the horrors of what the others must have endured?

I devoured every detail I could find, needing to know exactly what happened, while praying that Paul and the other two soldiers had not suffered in their final moments.

No wonder this was getting so much coverage back home. My survival *did* feel like a miracle.

Mom then showed me a few clips about candlelight vigils over the past twenty-four hours, as Americans prayed for me. My colleagues at CNN interviewed doctors and experts, where they discussed the extent of my injuries and the likelihood of a full recovery. All of this was interspersed with images and information about my professional and personal life. It was never ending, along with the homage paid to the others who had died.

I then clicked on a recent link that showed my doctor outside this very hospital, letting the reporters know that I was conscious and no longer in critical condition. He answered questions about my injuries and asked that our privacy, as a family, be respected. He thanked everyone for their interest and their prayers…

An hour later, the phone rang next to my bed, and it turned out to be a very surprising call.

I don't remember much about the conversation outside of the main points. I wish I had been a bit more coherent, but the morphine was still powerful in my system.

When I hung up, I blinked a few times and let my head fall back on the pillows, wondering if I had just dreamed that.

"Who was it?" Mom asked, recognizing that it was something significant.

I lifted my head off the pillow. "It was the president of CNN. He wanted to tell me personally how sorry he was about what happened."

"Isn't that nice," Mom said, reaching for Dad's hand and squeezing it.

"What else did he say?" Dad asked, knowing there was more.

I cleared my throat and let out a breath of disbelief. "He just offered me my own show. A full hour during prime time. He wants me to cover the hottest news stories of the day and go on location for the big stuff."

"No kidding!" Dad said. "Jack, that's incredible."

"He said I've been on their radar for a while, and that

my interviewing skills were top notch, but with all the publicity I've been getting, he thinks now's the time to launch me. He also asked if I'd be interested in being part of a documentary about what happened to me in Afghanistan—the bomb and my recovery."

"What would that involve?" Mom asked.

I was still thinking about whether or not I wanted to do it. I wasn't sure.

"A camera crew would come to the hospital and start right away, to interview me and stay with me over the next few weeks. I'm not sure about that part, because who would want to see me groaning? But he said the world wants to know me. And he wants me to start the show as soon as I'm able. But they're willing to wait, however long I need."

Mom got up, approached the bed and kissed me on the cheek. "No matter what you decide, it's a wonderful compliment. I'm proud of you."

"Will you do it, Jack?" Dad asked. "Will you take the job?"

"I told them that I'd think about it, but what's there to think about? The last thing he told me was the salary."

Mom's eyebrows lifted. "Will you get a raise?"

I laughed and realized it was the first time I'd cracked a smile since I woke up. "He said there's room for negotiation, but that it won't be less than seven figures annually, plus perks, including an apartment in New York until I find my own place. He said I'll be impressed with the view. Oh…and a full time driver."

Dad began to nod his head with a smile. "That all sounds pretty awesome."

I nodded in agreement. "Yes. It makes me want to get out of this bed right now and get back on my feet."

My dad stood up from his chair, approached the bed, and squeezed my hand. "You always were a fighter, Jack. I've never been more proud."

Aaron stood up as well and said with a nod, "Congratulations, Jack. Well deserved."

It was probably the first time in my life that I actually felt the past slip away and disappear completely. In that moment, Aaron was just my brother. Nothing more.

~ⒸⒸ

That night, after my parents left the hospital to check in at their hotel, I went to sleep thinking about what my mother had said when she first arrived—that my guardian angel must have been watching over me.

I couldn't help but float backwards in my mind to when I was just a boy of thirteen. I thought of Millicent Davenport and the year we spent together, and how my life was forever altered by our friendship.

We were never able to watch that movie, *Audrey Rose*, because when we returned to her house after building the first wall of our clubhouse, Millicent learned terrible news— that her grandmother in Arizona had just passed away.

I stood in the Davenport's kitchen, feeling like an intruder as they all wept and held each other. But then Millicent turned to me, strode across the floor, and threw her arms around my neck. She cried on my shoulder, and I held her tight.

The next day, I rode my bike to her house to say good-bye before they left for the airport.

"Remember your promise," she said to me in her bedroom, as she zipped up her suitcase. "You won't finish the clubhouse without me. You'll wait for me to come back."

"I will."

I couldn't believe she was going to be gone for two whole weeks. How would I live?

A short while later, I walked with her out the front door, carrying her suitcase for her. She paused on the sidewalk next to their minivan, put her hands on my shoulders and whispered in my ear, "Remember yesterday, when you said that you thought everyone was reincarnated?"

I nodded.

"Does that mean you think that I am, too?"

"Probably," I replied as I set her suitcase down on the curb.

She glanced over her shoulder at her younger sister, who was already buckled into the back seat. Millicent leaned closer and whispered in my ear again: "Did we know each other in a past life?"

I drew back and frowned at her for a moment, straining to remember. "I don't know," I replied. "I only remember little snippets of things every once in a while, but I kind of feel like this is the first time we've met. I don't feel that 'familiar' thing with you."

"Oh." Looking disappointed, she lowered her gaze. "I thought maybe we were soul mates or something."

I felt a rush of exhilaration at the suggestion, followed by the same flutter of nervous butterflies I had felt with Jeannie Morrison the previous fall. Suddenly, I found myself admiring Millicent's wavy, golden hair and thinking of how much I loved the dimples on both sides of her mouth when she smiled. Although she was not smiling now.

Not wanting her to leave town feeling disappointed, I said, "Maybe we are. Or maybe it's just new, and we've only just met for the first time."

Her sad eyes lifted, and she smiled at last. My heart pounded faster, and I wished she weren't leaving. All I wanted to do was go back to the clubhouse and talk to her about things I never talked about with other people.

"Yes," she said, "it must be new." Then she kissed me quickly on

the cheek and turned away, picking up her suitcase to throw into the back of the van.

She moved past me to get into her seat and then slid the door closed.

"Bye, Jack," she said, stretching her arm out the open window.

Her face was dazzling to me in that moment as I reveled in the sensation of her soft lips on my cheek. I couldn't speak. All I could do was back away from the curb and wave as she buckled her seat belt.

Her parents came out of the house and got into the van. They started up the engine, and again, I wished desperately that they weren't leaving. I could already feel a hole in my heart, because I was going to miss Millicent terribly, and her family, too.

"We'll see you soon, Jack," Dr. Davenport said, leaning across the seat to speak to me out the passenger side window. "Take care of yourself."

Then they drove off.

—❦—

That night in the hospital in Germany, I fell asleep remembering that special good-bye, followed by horror ten hours later when my mother hung up the telephone in our kitchen and turned to me. Her face was white as a sheet.

"What is it?" I asked, dread exploding like fire in my belly. "What's wrong?"

My mother moved slowly toward me and pulled a chair out to sit down at the kitchen table. She took both my hands in hers. "I have very bad news, Jack. There was a plane crash in Arizona."

My whole body went numb as I stared at her, not quite able to understand what she was trying to tell me.

"I'm so sorry." Her voice trembled, and her cheeks turned red. "Millicent won't be coming home."

"Why not?"

"Because her family was on that plane. They all died."

My heart beat like a hammer in my chest, and my blood churned thunderously in my ears. No, that wasn't possible.

"What do you mean? Why did the plane crash?"

She shook her head and pressed her fist to her mouth to stifle a sob. "I don't know. They're looking into it, but they think it was something mechanical. The plane caught fire and there was an explosion as they were landing. I'm sure we'll know more soon. We'll have to watch the news. I'm so sorry."

She reached forward to pull me into her arms. I shut my eyes, willing the words to be false. It wasn't true, I told myself. Millicent couldn't have been on that plane. She couldn't be dead. She was supposed to come home in two weeks. We'd promised each other that we would finish the clubhouse together.

"She was such a good girl," my mother said, rubbing her hand up and down my back. "They were a wonderful family. It's very tragic. I'm so sorry, Jack."

They were a perfect family, and I loved everything about them.

Tears spilled out of my eyes, and I clutched at my mother's shirt. "No!" I cried. "She was my best friend. I loved her."

My mother wept, too. "She was very special. And wherever she is right now, I'm sure she's watching over you, like a guardian angel. She'll always be with you, Jack."

I cried even harder.

As I lay in the hospital bed staring up at the ceiling, I couldn't help but wonder if my childhood friend had somehow been with me on that road in Afghanistan. Maybe she was responsible for the miracle that saved me.

Squeezing my eyes shut against the relentless pain, I told myself that if I ever met Millicent again in Heaven, I would be sure to thank her, and tell her how much I'd missed her.

PART II

CHAPTER

Eleven

Meg Andrews
2007

G rowing up, I never had much luck in the romance department and looking back on it, I don't know why I was in such a hurry to figure it all out. If only I had known that matters of the heart usually resolve themselves when the time is right. It just requires patience and the ability to follow your gut and listen to your intuition.

That was something I didn't know in my younger days, however, which is a bit surprising, considering I had an off-the-charts IQ. But nothing was easy back then when I was struggling to navigate my way through adolescence and the complicated politics of high school. Add to that my struggles with anxiety—a feeling of always needing to rush through things to get them done—and maybe because of that, it makes sense that I didn't have it all together.

Without a doubt, I was one of the nerdy girls—with braces, acne, straight A's and glasses. But the summer after graduation, just before I moved into residence at Princeton with a full academic scholarship, I decided I'd had enough of the life I was living, being reined in, and it was time for a fresh start. I went a little wild and got highlights in my hair. I watched *What Not To Wear* on TLC and figured out how to dress better. The braces finally came off, and I got contact lenses.

Being blond and pretty, for the first time in my life, boosted my confidence as I moved in at Princeton, but it wasn't easy to live up to the way I looked, because deep down, I was still a nerd at heart, anxious a lot of the time and definitely not one of the cool, laid-back girls.

I was brainy and uptight about my studies. Loud music in the dorm made me cranky and confrontational on a Friday night, and I often found myself storming out of my room to ask the offender to lower the volume. As a result, I spent most Friday nights in the library, because I could never be content with any grade less than an A.

That's not to say that the idea of going out wasn't a constant temptation. The girls on my floor were always trying to convince me to ditch the books and go out with them to parties or clubs. Occasionally I did, because I knew the importance of life experience outside of the classroom. I didn't want to be one of those "book-smart" people who had no idea how to survive in the real world.

And that's how I met Kyle—in the "real world" of college parties. He was impossibly handsome and popular, and didn't give a fig about his grades. A grade of C- was just fine with him.

Basically, he was the kind of guy I never imagined I would ever date.

As it turned out, I learned more from Kyle that year than I'd learned in any other year in my life, up to that point, so I can't regret it, no matter how disastrous it turned out to be.

~⊘

I'd never had a boyfriend in high school, and maybe that's why I was so easily seduced by Kyle—although that sounds like something out of a steamy romance novel. Maybe "insecure" more accurately describes the kind of person I was when I met Kyle at a dorm party during my third year.

I'll be honest and confess that I'd had too many beers that night. When he flirted with me, I was flattered, reckless, and uncharacteristically wild—and having been such a good girl all my life, I wanted to let loose, forget the worries for once, and have an adventure.

Kyle had dark hair and a muscular build, and I was bowled over by the power of my attraction to him. He also lived in a frat house, which all sounds terribly cliché, and sadly, it was. I'm not proud of it, but there it is. The fact that a guy like that wanted *me* was astounding. How was it possible that the geeky girl from Boise, Idaho had snagged one of the hottest guys at Princeton? I was privately high-fiving myself for weeks. That's how geeky I was.

Needless to say, while I fell head over heels in lust for the first time in my life, and actually started acting like a wild college girl, my grades went straight down the toilet—which wasn't a good thing for a female student trying to prove herself in the male-dominated mechanical engineering class. Before Kyle, I'd had no problem with that. I had the highest grades, well above all the guys.

But after six months of parties and pretending to be

something I wasn't, I had reached the end of the school year, barely hanging on to a B- average.

Heading into exams, I was completely stressed out.

That's when I came to my senses. It happened one night when Kyle dragged me out with his friends, and they all got drunk and wanted to tip over a mail box. I tried to talk them out of it because it was a federal offense, which only made them think it more hilarious. As I watched them do it, I could only shake my head. It was as if I had suddenly woken up from a deep slumber and realized I was in a place I didn't belong, hanging around with a bunch of idiots.

So there I stood the next morning, forty-eight hours before my first exam, outside the frat house, taking a deep breath and preparing myself to go inside and break up with my boyfriend.

~⊘

Truth be told, I always hated the inside of that house. It was dirty and smelled disgusting because the guys never said no to a party, and they seemed to have no idea how to put away garbage afterwards, clean a shower, or make a bed, let alone strip a bed and wash the sheets.

I had texted Kyle, so I knew he was there. He was in his room "studying," he said, but when I climbed the creaky staircase and knocked on his door, I found him lying on his bed with his earbuds in, drumsticks in hand, beating a tune on the air.

I walked in, and he pulled the buds out of his ears and sat up. "What's up?"

My stomach turned over with dread.

I didn't want to make a big deal out of this. I just

wanted it to be over so that I could get my head back in the game and study for exams without any distractions. Besides, I didn't think Kyle would care that much. He and I had had our share of fights and disagreements over the past few months, and lately he always seemed to be annoyed with me—criticizing everything I said and did—so I felt as if I were doing us both a favor.

"Listen…" I said, closing the door behind me and standing on the braided rug at the foot of his bed. The room reeked. I glanced around and spotted a pizza wrapper in the garbage can. He must have worked up an appetite the night before while tipping over the mail box.

The smell, mixed with the stench of stale beer in the dorm, was sickening. All I wanted in that moment was to be done with this, because we had nothing in common. I wasn't the blond party girl that Kyle thought I was. I wanted to get back to being the real me.

I cleared my throat and got straight to the point. "I don't know how to say this…but I think we both know this hasn't been working out lately. We've been getting on each other's nerves, and with exams coming up…"

Kyle frowned and sat up straighter on the bed. "What are you talking about? You haven't been getting on my nerves."

I hadn't? Then why did he always talk to me like I was stupid? No matter what I said or did.

I shifted testily on my feet and adjusted my backpack on my shoulder, and tried to speak lightly. "I just think we need to take a break. We both need to focus on exams."

Kyle swung his legs to the floor and sat on the edge of the bed, his hands curling tightly around the mattress. "Are you saying you want to break up?"

His expression was one of shock and disbelief, which made sense, considering he once told me he'd never been dumped. He'd always been the one to do the dumping.

Part of me was surprised he hadn't done it to me already, considering how critical he had become.

"Yes," I replied flatly.

Maybe I should have come up with a gentler way of putting it, or given him some hope for the future, even though I knew I wouldn't want to get back together with him, *ever*. Sure…it had been exciting at first, but now that the novelty had worn off, all I could see in front of me was a ridiculously great-looking guy who didn't care about school or responsibilities, or learning anything remotely academic. All that mattered to Kyle was the next party.

That wasn't the life I wanted.

Slowly, he stood up and approached me. For some reason, instinct compelled me to take a few steps back until I bumped into the door.

He frowned and shook his head at me. "I don't think you know what you're saying."

"I do," I insisted, feeling pressured to take it back.

He stared at me long and hard without saying a word. I felt trapped up against the door and my heart began to pummel my ribcage. There was something menacing about him that morning, and I couldn't say I'd been blind to it before. I'd always suspected some cruelty was there, simmering beneath the surface of his charm, but I'd chosen to ignore it because I was having fun most of the time, when he was charming.

Today, however, I felt uneasy. Swallowing hard, I wasn't sure what to expect from him. A muscle at his jaw twitched and a vein pulsed above his left eyebrow. He almost looked as if he might wrap his hands around my neck and choke me.

I glared at him, as if daring him to try something, praying he would step back.

Finally, he scoffed and turned away. I let out a deep breath as he flopped onto the bed and stuffed the earbuds into his ears again.

"You were a bore anyway," he said callously, closing his eyes and drumming the air. "Don't let the door hit you on the way out."

"Don't worry, I won't," I replied. "Have a good life."

Knowing he hadn't heard me because his music was so loud in his ears, I quickly turned, whipped the door open and hurried out into the corridor, where I smelled marijuana on the air, coming from one of the other bedrooms.

What was I doing there? How could I have thought this was where I was meant to be?

Dashing down the stairs, I reached the ground floor and ran outside to the street, not stopping until I made it to the sidewalk.

I didn't look back at the frat house as I walked briskly back to my dorm. Part of me was afraid Kyle might be watching me from the window. I certainly didn't want him to think I was harboring any regrets about breaking up with him, because if someone turned back the clock, I would do it again in a heartbeat.

My only regret was that for a few, irretrievable months, I'd lost sight of what mattered to me most—my studies, and the career I so desperately wanted.

CHAPTER

Twelve

That night, I sat at the desk in my room, studying with intense focus. The material, which I'd been ignoring all semester, covered fundamental laws of thermodynamics, waves and optics. I had to write this exam in less than thirty-six hours. At this point, every minute counted.

Coffee was a necessity. By 11:00 p.m., I was draining my third cup, staring into the empty bottom and wondering if I should make another. My logical brain weighed the pros and cons of that option. If I drank another, I probably wouldn't be able to fall asleep until dawn, and I knew the dangers of sleep deprivation to the human mind. I certainly didn't want to arrive at my exam with the shakes or an inability to focus. Sleep was important, so I tossed the cup into the trash can and reached for my water bottle instead.

A knock sounded at my door. Feeling slightly perturbed at the interruption, I rose from my desk to answer it.

As soon as I opened the door, my stomach dropped.

There stood Kyle, with red, puffy eyes, smelling of whisky. He was swaying on his feet, and I knew immediately that he was completely plastered.

"Meg," he sobbed, running a hand through his tousled, greasy hair and staggering to the side. "I'm sorry for what I said. You're the best, most beautiful girl I've ever known. You're not a bore."

At that moment, two doors swung open across the hall, and my neighbors leaned out to peer at me with annoyance. I couldn't blame them. It was exam week. No one had much patience for noisy drama in the hallway.

"Sorry," I said to them. "We'll be quiet." I grabbed Kyle by the wrist and pulled him into my room, shutting the door behind us. "People are trying to study."

He staggered toward my bed and fell face first onto it. For a few dire seconds I simply stared, worrying that he was going to pass out there for the entire night, and feeling positively enraged that he had come here, drunk, when we both had exams to study for. All I wanted to do was grab him by the jacket, drag him back outside, and tell him to go home and sober up. *Study, for pity's sake!* But I was not that heartless. I had to at least make an effort not to crush him completely.

Kyle rolled over and sat up on the edge of my bed. He clasped his hands together in his lap, looked up at me, then tears began to stream down his cheeks.

"I'm so sorry. Whatever I did, I won't do it again. I'll be better. I promise. Just tell me what it was."

"You didn't do anything wrong," I found myself saying, knowing that I couldn't be truthful with him right now. He wasn't in any state to discuss the nitty-gritty of our relationship, or what had been lacking. I couldn't tell him that I'd grown out of the "party-party" dynamic that was such a big part of who he was.

What I needed to do was talk him off the ledge and

convince him that he should go home and focus on studying for his exams.

"I must have done something wrong," he said, grabbing fistfuls of my shirt in his hands, pulling me toward him and pressing his cheek up against my belly, "or you wouldn't have broken up with me."

I didn't know what to say. He was completely different from the person he had been in the frat house earlier when he called me a bore.

All I could do was take hold of him and pull him to his feet. It wasn't easy. He was almost a dead weight.

He stared into my eyes with a muddled expression. I doubted he could even see straight. Then he drew me into his drunken embrace and slobbered in my ear. I smelled the heavy odor of booze on his breath, and it disgusted me.

"Please, don't end it, Meg. I can't live without you. You're the most amazing girl I've ever known. You're so smart," he argued, running his hands clumsily over my hair, kissing my forehead. "And you're so beautiful."

"I'm not so beautiful right now," I said, hoping to lighten the mood so I could just get rid of him. "I haven't brushed my teeth or washed my hair. I'm in study mode."

"That's what makes you so beautiful," he said, still stroking my head and face. "You're so brilliant."

Oh, God. I was certain he wouldn't remember any of this in the morning, so what was the point of this conversation when these were such important, precious hours? I couldn't let them go to waste. I had a whole semester of material to catch up on.

So I did what I had to do. I cupped Kyle's face in my hands and spoke firmly. "I didn't mean it," I said. "We don't have to break up. I just need some quiet time to study. That's all."

He stared into my eyes with the same inebriated, dazed expression, as if he didn't understand what I had just said. For a moment, I thought he might get angry, then his shoulders slumped with relief. "Do you mean it?"

"Of course," I replied. "But if we're going to work things out, I need you to understand and respect that I need these hours to hit the books. Please, Kyle. You understand, right?"

His speech was slurred. "That's why I love you, babe. Because you're such a brainiac. I respect that."

I laughed dutifully and tried to speak with a note of humor. "Well…if that's why you love me, then you have to let me study. I'll be mad if you don't."

He nodded and staggered backwards until he fell onto my bed, then he started laughing and couldn't stop.

I was breathing heavily by now, angry yet apprehensive, because I had no idea what he might do next. There was something so unpredictable about him.

Maybe it was selfish, but all I wanted was for him to leave me alone so I could get back to work. I would have said *anything* to make him go.

"What a klutz," Kyle said, fighting his way off the bed, then falling to the side and knocking over the lamp on my bedside table.

I grabbed hold of him and tried to help him to the door. "Will you be able to get home okay?" I asked. "And will you promise you'll study when you get back to your room? Make some coffee."

Of course I knew that such a suggestion was hopeless. He was far too drunk to retain any information, much less stay awake. He'd probably pass out the minute he fell onto his bed, if he even made it up the stairs.

It didn't matter. Failing exams was his problem. I just wanted him to leave.

Thank God, he did—but only after I let him kiss me good-bye in the hall.

As soon as I shut the door behind him, I used my sleeve to wipe his drunken kiss from my mouth, and picked my lamp up off the floor. I flicked the switch to make sure it still worked. Then I sat down on my bed for a long moment and rested my forehead on the heels of my hands, working hard to quell the anxiety that had risen in me during that encounter.

Finally, I got up and decided to pour another cup of coffee to make up for lost time.

I stayed up all night studying, catching only a few hours of sleep between 6 and 9 a.m. Then I left my room and found a quiet corner in the library to study all day—in a place where no one would find me.

Kyle texted me that afternoon and asked: *Are we good?*

Seated at a table in the library, I covered my face with both hands and shook my head. No, we weren't good, but I couldn't deal with him in that moment. I still had a lot of material left to cover, and I didn't want to mess up his game when he needed to be studying, too, so I quickly typed a reply: *Yes, we're good. I am studying the fundamentals of fluid power. You?*

He immediately replied: *Boring economics stuff.*

I didn't know what to say after that, but I knew it had to be something that would end the conversation, because I didn't want my phone to continue buzzing every five minutes that day.

Good luck! I texted. *Study hard!*

He replied with a smiling face icon, and I set my phone down on the table.

The rest of the day passed with no more texts from Kyle, nor did he show up at my door in another drunken stupor that night. I was relieved. And I hoped, for his own sake, that he was getting his act together and focusing on the books.

Just after I shut off the light in my room at 2:00 a.m., he sent me another text.

Good luck in the morning. I know you'll do great.

I decided not to reply. As far as Kyle knew, I was already asleep.

Shutting off my phone, I set it on the floor and pulled the covers up to my ears.

When I woke the following morning, I had only one thing on my mind—one single, vital goal: to write my exam and show my prof that I *did* deserve a place in his class, and that I was a strong enough candidate to be considered for the master's program.

Because when it came to mechanical engineering, I couldn't seem to get enough. I wanted to know everything there was to know about the field and reclaim my place at the top of my class.

As difficult as it had been lately, at least lessons were learned. It was time for me to focus on my future and stop trying to be something I was not.

I knew my purpose now.

And there was no place in my life for Kyle.

～☉

Unfortunately, Kyle didn't see it that way.

On the day I wrote my last exam, Kyle also wrote his. We both finished at noon, and he wasted no time before texting me from the frat house.

How'd you do?

A terrible feeling of dread washed over me because I knew I would have to break up with him all over again, after lying to him for the past week. I felt badly about that—

honestly I did. It brought me no pleasure to hurt him, but I also believed I had done the right thing by helping him to stay focused on school and encouraging him to study for his exams. Heaven knew where he might be right now if I'd insisted on a clean break the night he came to my room. He might still be drunk.

I texted him back. *It was rough. How about you?*

It was okay. Glad to be done. Time to celebrate. Want to meet me for lunch at the pub?

I took a deep breath and thought about it for a few seconds, and couldn't see any way around it. I would have to see him and put an end to our relationship—*today*—before I boarded my flight home at 7:00 p.m.

At least my departure would force a physical separation between us over the summer. Our relationship would simply die a slow, gradual death and Kyle would have time to get over me and hook up with some other girl—as I was certain he would. He was incredibly good looking and he knew how to pour on the charm. As soon as he hit the beaches in South Carolina, he'd be snatched up within a week by a girl who would most likely be a much better match.

But still… I had an unpleasant task before me and had to get over that hurdle. I had to explain to Kyle how I really felt, and make it clear that I didn't want to maintain a long-distance relationship over the summer.

As I texted him back and suggested that we meet in the cafeteria—because I didn't have much time; I still had to pack up my room and sign out of residence—I felt almost sick to my stomach. I couldn't imagine any day more stressful than this one. Not only had it started out with an exam I wasn't ready for, but now I had to break up with my unpredictable boyfriend. For the second time.

I just hoped nothing would cause me to miss my flight, because there was nothing I wanted more than to get on that plane, buckle in, and get that nightmare over with, too.

Fourteen

I hate to admit this, after everything I just revealed about myself, but when I got off the plane in Boise, after surviving the break-up in the cafeteria, I was completely bombed. Blitzed, sozzled, tanked-up, and every other word you can think of to describe a young woman of diminutive size who had consumed too much alcohol at high altitudes.

You see...not only had I just made it through one of the most stressful days of my life, but I always had a terrible fear of flying. Just getting seated on any airplane was enough to give me a coronary.

As soon as I boarded, I quietly explained my nervousness to the flight attendant, who was kind enough to discreetly spot me a couple of tiny bottles of vodka, which I guzzled in front of the overweight businessman who sat next to me in the window seat.

"I'm so sorry about this," I said to him, after I sucked down the first bottle and grimaced at the scalding sensation in my throat. "I hate flying."

"That should take the edge off," he replied with a chuckle. "But really, you have nothing to worry about. Air travel is safer than driving."

I nodded my head and unscrewed the tiny cap on the second bottle. "Believe me, I know all the stats. I've studied them from top to bottom. But it doesn't make me feel any less relaxed during takeoff. Don't even get me started about the landing."

I paused for a few seconds, then tipped up the second bottle and drank half of it. I forced myself to keep the rest for when we began taxiing toward the runway.

"Normally, I'm a very rational person," I told him. "I'm an engineering student, so I'm totally into science and stats, but for some reason, none of my self-talk or any empirical evidence makes a lick of difference when I step on one of these giant death machines. All I can think about is the terror of rapid descent. Sorry," I said, realizing I probably wasn't helping his mood any.

"No worries," he replied, sitting forward and speaking calmly. "I've been a frequent flier for twenty years. Nothing scares me now."

"Knock on wood when you say that," I warned him, "because if you've been that lucky for that long, the odds could be stacked against you." I shut my eyes and slapped my forehead with the palm of my hand. "Geez, just tell me to shut up. That was a stupid thing to say. It's been a rough day."

"Don't apologize," he said, leaning back. "And don't worry. Everything's going to be fine."

I knew he was just trying to be helpful, but I hated when people said that to me on flights, because how could they know everything was going to be fine? No one had a crystal ball.

Happily, the plane didn't crash, and by the time the pilot announced that we were beginning the descent, I was half in the bag, sound asleep with earplugs in. The man beside me had the sense not to wake me, and my eyes flew open only when the wheels touched down.

At least, by that point, there was no time in advance for my anxiety to get a foothold. I just clutched the seat in front of me, grit my teeth, and breathed a heavy sigh of relief when we slowed down a few seconds later and began to taxi toward the gate.

The alcohol had helped. It had knocked me out like a sledgehammer. It was a good thing I didn't fly very often, or I might have a drinking problem.

A short while later, as I approached the baggage carousel and spotted my brother who had come to pick me up, I spread my arms wide and grinned. "I'm alive!"

He laughed and strode forward to hug me. "And self-medicated, I see." He held me tight for a long moment, then drew back. "You look great, even if you can't count how many fingers I'm holding up." He held up two.

"Peace," I said, returning the gesture. "And you don't know the half of it." I was very aware that I was slurring my consonants, but it was past midnight, and Wayne loved me unconditionally, so I didn't worry about it. "You wouldn't believe the day I had."

"Tell me all about it." He took me by the arm and led me toward the baggage carousel.

~*O*

Interestingly enough, my half-brother Wayne was a pilot with a major commercial airline. He was ten years older than me, and had always been my hero, because he'd been taking care of me since before I could walk. My parents had both worked. It was a second marriage for them, and I was the only child from their second kick at the can, which turned out to be more successful than the first. At least that's what the evidence suggests, because there they were, still together after twenty-two years, and very much in love.

But back in those early years, Wayne had often been charged with the duty of babysitting, which, as far as I know, he never complained about.

I loved him more than anyone on the planet.

"So what happened with Kyle?" he asked, because I had already told him about the break-up that hadn't stuck the first time.

"It was ugly," I replied. "He wanted to go to a pub for lunch to celebrate being done exams, but I convinced him to meet me at the cafeteria because I wanted to be in a public place, on campus."

Wayne frowned. "Were you worried he'd get violent?"

I shrugged. "I don't know. Maybe."

The other passengers from my flight were all crowded around the carousel, waiting for the bags to come down. I made eye contact with the businessman who had sat next to me, and he gave me a nod from the opposite side of the carousel. I smiled and waved.

I turned back to Wayne. "So we got our lunches at the counter, and I waited until we were done eating before I dropped the bomb. Then it was brutal."

"What did you say to him?"

"I tried to be gentle about it. I said it wasn't him, it was me, and that I just wanted to take a break over the summer and see how we both felt in the fall."

"So he still has hope."

I shook my head. "I don't think so, because he didn't take it too well. He got angry and accused me of being a tease over the past week, stringing him along when I knew full well that I wasn't going to give it a second chance. He called me selfish and shallow. Then he called me the B word and a bunch of other profanities before he shoved his plate across the table, spilling my water all over my lap."

Wayne shook his head and regarded me intensely. "You don't deserve to be treated like that. No one does. You're better off without him."

"Believe me, I know."

The baggage carousel came on just then, and bags started sliding down the conveyor belt. All the passengers perked up and began to pay attention.

"I'd love to get my hands on that turkey head," Wayne said. "If I had been there, I would have kicked him in the you-know-what."

I watched for my suitcases. "That would have been fun to see, but I had it covered. I wasn't going to back down. After he spilled the water on me, I said, 'So I guess we're done now,' and he said, 'I guess we are.' Then he got up and walked out on me, and I haven't heard a word from him since. He drives home to South Carolina with a couple of guys tomorrow morning, so I'm sure they'll be partying and picking up women the whole way. He'll forget about me soon enough."

"I hope so," Wayne said, pointing toward one of my suitcases. "Is that yours?"

A short while later, we were seated in his truck with all my bags, heading home. I couldn't wait to sleep in my own bed.

We barely made it two miles beyond the airport when my cell phone buzzed and a long text came in.

"Ah, shoot," I said to Wayne as I read it.

He glanced at me from behind the wheel. "What is it?"

"It's Kyle." I let out a deep breath, feeling completely sober all of a sudden. "I guess he doesn't know the meaning of the word 'done.'"

Scrolling through the message, I felt my heart begin to pound.

Kyle must have been drunk and talking trash about me with his friends all night. They had probably worked him up into a tizzy, because the text was a series of insults and expletives, calling me every name in the book, and because Kyle knew about my fear of flying, he said he hoped my plane crashed. He even described all the things that could go wrong, and told me to imagine how it would feel when the plane hit the ground like a speeding bullet and burst into flames.

My stomach clenched tight and I asked Wayne to pull over. He was quick to respond, and within seconds, I was spilling out of the car and retching onto the shoulder of the road.

Wayne shut off the engine, got out, and hurried to my side to hold my hair back. "You'll be all right," he said, rubbing my back. "Except that you'll be a little hungover tomorrow, that's all."

I was aware of cars speeding past on the road and the smell of new asphalt. After a moment, I collected myself, straightened, and wiped at my burning, watery eyes.

"It's not just that," I replied. "It was the text he wrote. You should read it."

Wayne shook his head with annoyance and leaned into the truck to reach for my phone. He read the whole message and turned to me. "Mind if I reply?"

I waved a hand through the air and leaned back against the side of his truck. "Knock yourself out."

Wayne typed a message, pressed send, and showed it to me.

Hey Kyle. This is Meg's brother, Wayne. You're a dick. Stop texting my sister and see if it's possible for you to act like a grown-up.

I read it and chuckled. "You're my superhero. Thank you."

"He really is a dick. What did you ever see in him?"

I shrugged. "I don't know. It was temporary insanity, I suppose, because he was so good looking. He's just the kind of guy I've always found attractive... Dark hair, blue eyes."

"Beauty is only skin deep," Wayne said, handing back my phone. "It's the soul that matters. And if he texts you back, don't reply. Just ignore him. Do not engage. He'll eventually get tired of badgering you and move on."

Wayne ushered me into the truck and shut the door. Then he returned to the driver's seat, started the engine, checked the side mirror and steered us back onto the road.

Another text came in, and it said only one thing: *F.U.*

"Nice," I said. "I sure can pick 'em."

~ ⊘

Kyle continued to try and contact me over the next few days, but it wasn't what I expected. The following morning, he actually called my cell phone, but I chose not to answer it. He then had no choice but to send a string of texts where he apologized profusely for the things he had said, and begged me to talk to him. He promised it would never happen again. He promised he would never hurt me or say anything so stupid or mean.

But I remembered his false promises on the night he came to my dorm room. It was obvious that he wasn't someone I could ever trust or depend on, and his volatile behavior was not something I wanted in my life.

I wanted to follow Wayne's advice and not respond, but after about twenty messages, I felt it would be best to put Kyle out of his misery and accept his apology, but be firm about my decision. All I wanted was for him to move on. I wanted to be free of him.

I accept your apology, Kyle. Thank you. I appreciate that. But I'm sorry… I don't want to get back together. We're not right for each other. You know it as well as I do. Take the summer to forget about us and move on. Please don't text me anymore. It's over.

To my surprise, he didn't reply. Not even a simple *OK* to acknowledge my message.

I decided to leave it at that, feeling thankful—and hopeful—that I wouldn't have to deal with any more drama, and that I wouldn't receive another abusive text the next time he went out with the boys and got hammered.

～⊘

The next four weeks passed uneventfully, with no more texts or calls from Kyle, and it was pure heaven to know that he was on the other side of the country. I didn't care what he was doing or who he was seeing. In fact, I hoped he'd found a new girlfriend and was madly in love with her, and was now wondering what he'd ever seen in me. That would be just fine, because I had met someone myself—a young man who was the exact opposite of Kyle…fair hair, tall lanky build, and obsessed with school, just like me.

His name was Malcolm. I met him at my summer job as a waitress in a high-end downtown restaurant. Malcolm was a physics grad who had just been accepted into medical school in San Diego. He'd been hired as a waiter for the summer, working the dinner hour.

Malcolm was brilliant, academically speaking, and he never flew off the handle or wanted to tip over a mailbox. He was a grown-up, and very driven and ambitious. That was one of the things I loved most about him, because I was happy being the same way.

We started dating after about three weeks of working together, and by August, things had gotten pretty serious. My family thought he was a healthy change after Kyle, and their approval mattered to me a great deal.

The only problem was that Malcolm was about to start medical school on the West Coast, while I was heading back east to finish the final year of my engineering degree at Princeton, and possibly do a master's. I was disappointed that we wouldn't be able to spend more time together because I believed he might actually be "the one." I didn't want to break up, but I knew that if we were going to see each other during the school year, I would have to get over my fear of flying.

Was that even possible? I was uneasy as the end of August approached—because I'd never been able to talk myself out of that fear in the past.

"You should let me take you flying and give you some lessons," Wayne said one afternoon when he was home for four days after a few flights back and forth to Europe. We had just gotten into his truck to drive to the supermarket and pick up some steaks for the barbeque. "We could go to the flying club and you can sit in the cockpit with me, and I'll let you steer the plane and hold the yoke."

He backed out of the driveway and started off down the street.

"Are you joking?" I replied. "You're talking about a small, private plane? I'd rather stick needles in my eyes."

"No, you wouldn't," Wayne replied. "I promise, you'll love it, and I'll be right there, beside you the whole time. And I know you, Meg. When you want to accomplish something, you attack it, hard. So attack this. You just need to face your fear and feel like you're in control." He glanced at me from behind the wheel as he drove onto the main road. "I'm ninety-nine percent sure that when you're sitting in the captain's seat, and you see how it all works, you'll be hooked."

"I don't know," I said hesitantly, gazing off at the mountains in the distance.

Wayne reached across the seat and squeezed my shoulder. "Come on, it'll be fun. Just give it a try. We could go tomorrow."

I breathed deeply as I held my arm out the open window and felt the lift of the wind beneath my palm. I couldn't deny that something in me had always been fascinated by the science of aerodynamics and the fact that a giant 400-ton machine could even get off the ground.

At the same time, any news about a major air disaster left me morbidly captivated and glued to the television set. I would read everything I could get my hands on about it. I wanted to know exactly what had happened, and more importantly, *why* it happened.

Maybe Wayne was right. Maybe I just needed to face my fear head on. Maybe even embrace it.

"Okay," I said with purpose, turning to look at him. "Let's do it. Can we make it happen tomorrow?"

Just saying the words sent a burst of adrenaline into my veins.

Wayne grinned at me, looking very pleased. "I'll see what I can do, Captain Andrews."

PART III

Nine Years Later

Jack Peterson

I always knew when rain was in the forecast. I didn't need a meteorologist to tell me about it, because I felt it in my right knee and thigh, and sometimes in my arm.

As I sat at my mother's kitchen table at her summer house in Cape Elizabeth, Maine, after my parents had gone to bed, I massaged my right quadriceps. Though the femur was completely healed and I had no trouble walking, it was a bone-deep ache on days like this, when bad weather was coming.

For a moment, I considered taking something for it, but decided against that because this was nothing, really. Nothing compared to those early weeks in the German hospital after the bombing, which included a second surgery to replace my knee and a full schedule of excruciating physio that lasted for many months back home in the United States. Not to mention the burns on my chest and stomach which took forever to heal.

At any rate, I had been on pain killers for a full year, and it hadn't been easy to get off them, which was why I rarely took anything for pain these days. This level of discomfort, I could handle.

Rising from my chair, I carried my phone out to the front deck overlooking the water, and sat down on one of the Adirondack chairs. I tipped my head back to look up at the stars, but there were no stars that night because of low cloud cover. I couldn't see the moon either. Nevertheless, it was a warm and windless night. Wonderfully tranquil. Just the sound of the waves lapping onto the beach and the salty scent of the sea made it worth the trip from Manhattan that afternoon.

I wondered what Katelyn and Aaron were up to in Portland. I hadn't even told Katelyn I was flying home for the weekend, because that had been a rather spontaneous decision. It had been a slow news week with not much happening in the world, so it seemed like a good time to get out of the city.

By now, it was almost 10:00 p.m., and I wondered if it was too late to call.

I decided to text Katelyn to find out what they were up to tomorrow.

Hey there. Surprise—I'm in Cape Elizabeth. You still up?

I set the phone down on the arm of the chair and wondered if things would ever change. Would there ever come a day when my brother's wife wouldn't be the main reason I wanted to get on a plane and fly home for a visit— even when I knew she would always love Aaron, and that she and I would never be anything but friends?

At least, since I'd returned home from Afghanistan, I'd finally come to terms with it. I'd learned to accept things the way they were. Life was rough. There it was in a nutshell. And never in a thousand years would I want to jeopardize what she and Aaron had, or cause tension in their family. I loved Katelyn and the kids too much.

As for Aaron, beneath the civility, he and I still didn't like each other a whole lot—because not all memories could be swept under the carpet—but neither of us wanted our age-old issues to infect the rest of the family, the kids especially.

I had no children of my own and I wanted to be a good uncle to them, and of course, I wanted Katelyn to be happy. I believe that was Aaron's priority as well—which I respected, because we both loved her—so we found a way to lay the past to rest. At least on the surface.

My phone rang just then. I picked it up and saw that it was Katelyn. "Hello?"

"Hey stranger," she said. "When did you get in?"

I closed my eyes for a second and wallowed in that familiar sense of calm, because for some reason, just the sound of Katelyn's voice made everything feel right with the world.

"A few hours ago. It was a last-minute decision. I thought I might go out with Dad and do some sailing, but that was before I realized it was going to be raining all weekend."

"Yes, they're calling for some bad weather," she said. "But it's not supposed to start until tomorrow afternoon. You could always get out there early."

"Maybe." Though I didn't feel terribly inspired.

"How's everything at work?" she asked.

Like me, Katelyn was a reporter and was currently lead anchor for the evening news at one of the local Portland stations. She was a celebrity in town, and it didn't hurt that she was married to the richest man in Maine—the man who built the boat that won the most recent race for the America's Cup.

"It's been a slow month for news," I replied, "which isn't a bad thing, I suppose."

"I hear you," she said. "No major disasters or embarrassing political scandals. We should be thankful."

"But where's the fun in that?" I said, and she laughed.

"Would you like to come for dinner tomorrow night?" she asked. "The kids would love to see you. Invite Margie and Stan, too."

"They just went to bed," I replied, "but I'll mention it in the morning."

"Great," she said. "Well, I should get going. It's late. I'll tell Aaron you're in town, and we'll see you around five tomorrow?"

"Sounds good. I'll see you then."

I ended the call, set my phone down on the arm of the wooden chair, and sat for a while on the front deck, alone, listening to the waves and staring out at the dark water.

Eventually, I noticed that the world had become abnormally quiet. The crickets stopped chirping, and there wasn't a breath of wind in the air. It felt almost eerie, and I sat forward, listening intently, my eyes focused and alert.

Nothing.

The pain in my leg returned, so I massaged the muscle with the heel of my hand, then rose from the chair to go back inside.

If only I had known, then, what was to come—that there would be no joyful family dinner with Katelyn and Aaron the next day. I would not see the children and build houses out of LEGO with them on their family room floor, nor would we eat ice cream with sprinkles on their veranda overlooking the city.

Within hours, there would only be chaos.

CHAPTER

Seventeen

Shortly after I went inside the house, I turned on the television and sat down on the sofa in the front room. I lowered the volume so as not to wake my parents, and scrolled mindlessly through the guide, searching for a good film.

I remember precisely what time it was at that point, because I had checked the clock on my phone, which indicated 10:17 p.m.

About ten seconds later, a terrible noise erupted somewhere, far off in the distance. I stood up instantly, moved to the window, pulled the curtains aside, and looked out.

It sounded like thunder, but I knew it was nothing of the kind.

My stomach dropped—a typical response for me, because I'd suffered some post-traumatic stress after my accident. A sudden loud noise would often cause me to jump and relive the terror of the Hummer flipping over repeatedly on the road in Afghanistan.

But it had been nine years since then, and I was mostly over it. On that particular night at the window in my parents' living room, I knew, intellectually, that I was not in the middle of a war. I was in Cape Elizabeth, enjoying the peace and quiet of the seaside community that was like a second home to me.

Although it was not so peaceful at 10:17 p.m.

The noise grew louder, and the walls began to shake. I quickly grabbed my phone and pressed record. I filmed the vase teetering on the coffee table and noticed the lights starting to flicker.

"Mom, Dad! Get up!"

My father ran out to the front room, tying the belt on his navy terrycloth bathrobe. "What is it?"

"I don't know yet." I ran to the kitchen and whipped open the front door, recording everything the entire time. I stepped onto the deck with my father close behind me. We both looked up to find the sky over our heads bright orange.

"Oh, no," I said, filming the glowing clouds, wondering if we should go back inside or run for our lives.

"What's happening?" Dad asked, staring upward with wide eyes.

My mother shouted at us from behind the screen door. "Get inside!" She opened the door, reached out and tried to pull me back by the fabric of my shirt. I stumbled as I fought to keep my camera focused on the sky.

The house began to shake, and the terrifying noise was back, only it was different this time, as fire and fragments of steel and metal began to rain down onto the beach and into the shallow waters in the cove.

"I'm standing on my deck in Cape Elizabeth, Maine," I said for the benefit of the camera, "recording something that appears to have exploded in the sky."

A sudden gust of wind rose up and nearly knocked me over, and I felt the heat from the firestorm.

The noise became deafening as a huge silver engine dropped out of the sky and landed on the beach with a thunderous impact, causing the sand to splash up like water. I was too stunned to comment on what it might be, although I was certain it was a commercial jet engine.

Half a second later, another structure crashed to earth, landing in the wooded area just behind the Kettle Cove parking lot. The ground shook beneath my feet, and I had to shield my eyes from the wind, dust, and burning sparks that flew toward the house. Bits of red-hot metal tore through the air, barraging cars and lighting wooden fences on fire.

When I uncovered my eyes, I recognized what had landed in the trees: the front half of a giant commercial airliner. Around me, the neighborhood was burning, people were running and screaming, and I felt as if I were standing in the middle of the apocalypse.

All I could do was leap over the deck rail with my camera still running. I began to describe what I was witnessing as I sprinted toward the crash site where the fuselage had landed.

CHAPTER

Eighteen

Meg Andrews

National Transportation Safety Board Headquarters
Washington, D.C.

"Did any of it go down in the water?" I asked Gary, the investigator in charge, as I followed him down the hall to his office.

Every phone at every desk was ringing, and the office had gone from quiet to complete pandemonium in a matter of minutes. The other on-call members of the Go Team were still arriving, but I had been in the office from the outset, working late, polishing the prose on my section of an open accident report.

When Gary called me on my cell to ask me to come in right away, I told him I was already there.

"Why aren't I surprised?" he asked with a defeated sigh. "Go turn on CNN, Meg. There's been an accident with Jaeger-Woodrow Airways—Flight 555. I'll see you in fifteen minutes."

Since that moment, I had been on the telephone, fielding calls from the media and different government authorities. I had never been so glad to see Gary walk through the door. He was a tall, large African American man in his early sixties, with a voice like James Earl Jones. As soon as he entered a room, it felt like everything was about to be wrestled under control.

On top of all that, he was like a father to me.

"That's what's still not clear," he replied as he moved behind his desk, sat down and booted up his computer. "From the video, it looks like some of it went down in the water just off the beach, and other parts, on land. And there are some reports of more wreckage a mile or two off the coast, which suggests the fuselage broke apart at high altitude, long before impact. Those are rough waters off Cape Elizabeth, so the crash site will be a challenge, if that's what happened."

"So there might have been an explosion," I said, already considering the implications of that.

Gary gave me a look. "You know better than that, Meg. Don't make any assumptions until you see the evidence."

"I know, I know," I said. "I'm just eager to get there."

"Me, too. Hannah's working on our flights and hotel rooms, and we need to find a suitable location to set up command headquarters. You can help out with that. You know the drill. We'll need plenty of phone lines and scanners." His cell phone rang and he checked the call display. "Shit. It's the FBI. I have a feeling this one's going to be complicated." Before he answered the call, he waved a hand to usher me out of his office. "Keep your eye on CNN and everything Jack Peterson is reporting. He saw the whole thing and he's right there. Let me know if they find any survivors."

I hurried out of Gary's office.

While I worked at getting our team assembled to leave for the crash site, I continued to watch CNN, and was amazed at the footage Jack Peterson had managed to capture—which they replayed constantly, over and over—not to mention the fact that the plane had gone down, practically in his front yard. At times I had to stop, shut everything out, and focus my eyes on the television screen, because I was a structures specialist and the footage was giving me a sense of the timing and direction of the aircraft's fall from the sky.

I was looking to determine how much of the plane was intact when it impacted the ground. I listened carefully to the roar of the engine just before it landed—which suggested that the problem had not been engine failure. But we wouldn't know anything for sure until we arrived on site and the systems specialists got to work on the evidence.

There was no question in my mind that we were going to need a copy of that video, so our specialists could analyze every detail.

It was now 11:25 p.m., and Peterson was broadcasting live from the site with a professional cameraman and a satellite van nearby. He was capturing more footage of the firefighters combing through the wreckage for survivors, all the while speculating about what might have caused the crash.

"So far, we don't know exactly what happened here, but based on reports from eyewitnesses, myself included, it appears that there was an explosion, which occurred while the plane was still in the air. We do not yet know if there was some sort of explosive device on board, or if it was caused by a mechanical issue. We hope we will have those answers soon, when the investigators arrive. But the first priority is, of course, the continuing search for survivors."

I shook my head at him, wishing he wouldn't start suggesting that there might have been a bomb on board, when we had no idea—at least not yet—what happened, or why. The last thing we needed was the media fanning flames of panic and suspicion before we even got there.

As far as survivors were concerned…

Based on what I had seen so far, I knew there was very little possibility that anyone could have survived that crash. Although, I never stopped praying for miracles.

Just then, the phone rang at my desk. It was Gary. "We have a government plane waiting for us on the tarmac," he said. "Grab your bag and tell the others. It's time to go."

"I'm on it."

With all the chaos in the office, I realized I hadn't yet called Malcolm to let him know I was leaving town. I felt guilty for a moment, for not thinking of him right away, but then I brushed that off because he rarely called me either, when things got crazy for him at work.

Sometimes I wished it were different between us, but this was the way it was.

At any rate, I was relieved when I called his number and it went straight to voicemail, because I didn't have time to chat.

Nineteen

The flight from Washington to Portland would last about ninety minutes, and Gary insisted that all members of the team try and get some sleep. He was a stickler about that and believed none of us would be any good to the investigation if we couldn't think properly because of sleep deprivation.

Knowing that I would have to hit the ground running, I tried to close my eyes after takeoff, but couldn't—because despite the fact that I had conquered my fear of flying and had logged nearly 2000 hours as a pilot myself, my heart still raced whenever I felt an aircraft pick up speed on the runway and lift off the ground.

So instead of relaxing and falling asleep, I found myself discreetly opening my laptop and slipping my headphones on to watch Jack Peterson reporting from the crash site.

It was odd, how he always reminded me of Kyle, my first real boyfriend in college. Jack had the same dark hair and similar facial features, the same muscular build and physical charisma. He even sounded the same when he spoke.

But that's where the resemblance ended, because Jack

Peterson was an extraordinarily intelligent man with class and sensitivity. There was something mature and worldly about him. He was the polar opposite of Kyle in every other way.

Beauty is only skin deep. It's the soul that matters.

Sometimes I wondered whatever became of Kyle after graduation. Maybe he eventually grew up and stopped tipping over mail boxes. It was just college after all—a time for us to spread our wings, experiment a little, and figure out who we truly were.

That's what I had done. I came out of my shell and figured it out.

Maybe one of these days, I would look Kyle up on Facebook, just out of curiosity.

But not today. There were other more pressing matters on my mind.

I watched Jack Peterson for the duration of the flight, and just before landing, I felt a sick knot in my belly as he spoke about a teddy bear he found in the wreckage, not far from the burned body of a young child.

At that point, Jack paused, swallowed hard, and turned his face away from the camera. He bowed his head and exhaled sharply, cleared his throat and then collected himself, faced the camera again, and continued.

Something in me broke apart in that moment, and I swallowed over a jagged lump of sorrow that rose in my throat.

The female anchor at the news desk at the CNN station was sympathetic. They took him off the live feed and switched to another reporter at the Portland Head Light Museum, where a number of news vans were set up to report on the search over the water. Helicopters circled overhead, shining lights on the black ocean. Local fishermen and yachtsmen had also volunteered to aid in the search.

I felt for Jack Peterson, because I knew exactly what it was like to work on a crash site where you had to force yourself to detach emotionally from the stressful, disturbing reality of what you were seeing—because you had a job to do. An important job.

But every once in a while, something hit home, and it would crush you.

I was fully aware that Jack Peterson was a man who had witnessed his own share of trauma and disaster. We'd all watched him recover from that near-fatal bombing in Afghanistan. Ever since that day, he'd become one of America's favorite sons and a prominent host at CNN.

In that regard, his fame didn't surprise me at all. Not only was he handsome, intelligent and charismatic, but there was something accessible about him. I think everyone in the country felt a connection to him. I certainly did.

Sometimes, when he spoke directly into the camera— which he always did as host of the news show—I felt as if he were speaking directly to me, and that he was a cherished friend I'd known forever. I'd seen him in the hospital, after all. We'd *all* seen him.

We'd all been there when he recovered from multiple surgeries and took his first steps. We saw his burn scars and felt his pain.

It was strange to imagine that I might meet him in person in a few short hours.

If I did, I would thank him for capturing the footage of the crash, which would be a crucial element to help us piece together what had happened, exactly.

So there it was… He was a hero again, because with the

help of that footage, we would have concrete evidence to help us form stronger conclusions and make recommendations to the FAA—to prevent this from happening again.

That was what mattered most to me. It was why I was so passionate about this job.

A short while later, our jet touched down in Portland. We all quickly gathered up our things and prepared to travel to the crash site.

~*⊘*

"Hey Reynolds! The tin-kickers are here!" one of the FBI guys said as we got out of our rental cars. We all wore navy jackets with NTSB emblazoned on the backs, so we were easily identifiable.

I gave Gary a look because I knew he hated that term, but I didn't mind it. That's what we did—we used our boots to flip over pieces of wreckage to search for what clues lay beneath.

While Gary consulted with the FBI guys—they were the lead agency because of the potential criminal element—I strolled across the parking lot to see what I could.

The sun was just coming up and the morning sky was overcast. A thick fog had rolled in off the water, which seemed to accentuate the heavy smell of aviation fuel in the air. The parking lot was full of cop cars, fire trucks, and ambulances, all with lights flashing. As I made my way past them, I worked hard to control the pace of my breathing, to prepare myself for what I was about to behold.

I circled around the back of a fire truck and the main crash site, shrouded in pale gray fog, came into view.

Stopping on the pavement, I took a deep breath, then

another and another to keep my stress symptoms at bay, while I observed the vast area of devastation and wreckage. The enormous front half of the jet was relatively intact, but the interior was completely burned out. The hull was slashed open by the trees, which were now flattened beneath it. Behind the fuselage, the crash path had created an elongated crater in the earth.

The back half and tail had broken off and fallen in some other location. There was no sign of the wings anywhere.

Thousands of pieces of fragmented metal, battered luggage, and scorched airline seats were strewn across the smoldering field, or hanging from branches in trees on either side of the crash path.

There were also bodies. A number of them. Seeing them caused that familiar pain in my chest, and I breathed deeply again. I let it out slowly.

Breathe, Meg. Just breathe.

It always struck me as disrespectful, not to remove the bodies sooner, but I understood that because it was a criminal investigation, all the passengers were considered potential murder victims, and they were part of the crime scene. They simply could not be removed until investigators had a chance to document every last detail. This was why the press was restricted from the immediate area for now, and no one was allowed past the barricades to film or take pictures—outside of the proper authorities.

As I stood on the edge of the parking lot, striving to maintain my composure, my body went numb and still—as if all my internal organs had stopped functioning to allow for a moment of silence. Every part of me needed to mourn for these poor lost souls, and I prayed they were long gone from this dreadful place.

It was always like this for me. Whenever I stepped onto a crash site, I needed to wrestle my anxiety under control. Then I would take a moment to comprehend the enormity of what I was seeing. I had to do all of that before I could wake up the part of my brain that had to be inquisitive and academic.

First, I had to seek calm. Only then, could I get to work.

It was a long day at the main crash site as I examined what remained of the fuselage and cockpit, and searched through as much wreckage as I could, turning things over, taking pictures of everything, from every possible angle. Other members of my team were on the beach where the engine had landed, and still others had gone out on the water where they were working with the Coast Guard to search for the rest of the wreckage, including the tail. That's where they hoped to find the black box.

No one had found the wings yet, which was where the fuel tanks had been located—an important element of the investigation, given that there had been an explosion in the air.

And that's what made it challenging on this first day. The plane had broken apart at 30,000 feet while traveling over 500 miles per hour, and so the crash area was spread across many miles, including the ocean.

A short while ago, a rescue worker informed me that a man had called in to report an airline seat hanging from a tree in his backyard, sixty miles away.

Clearly, we were going to be in Maine for a while.

By mid-afternoon, Gary brought Carol—another NTSB colleague of ours, in charge of public affairs—across the debris-strewn crash site to find me. I was standing in front of the nose at that point, inspecting the exterior.

"Hey, Meg," Gary said. "We have a chopper lined up to do another sweep, and I thought you'd like to go, to see what everything looks like from the sky."

"That would be great," I said.

"Can you come right now?" he asked. "The chopper's on its way to the parking lot at Crescent Beach, and we have a car waiting to take you there."

"No problem." I packed up my gear bag and followed them off the crash site. We got into a black SUV with Gary and me riding in the back seat, and Carol sitting in front.

After we pulled out of the barricaded lot, we drove past about thirty TV news vans with satellite dishes on their rooftops. There were cameras and news crews everywhere, from local and national stations. I found myself searching the logos for CNN.

"It's quite the spectacle, isn't it?" Carol said, turning in her seat to look back at me as I peered out the window.

"It certainly is."

"That's actually what I wanted to talk to you about," Carol said, hesitantly.

I pulled my gaze from the window to pay closer attention to her, because it was her job to deal with the media, and I wasn't quite sure why she was even here in this vehicle with *me*, when there were press conferences to attend and multiple debriefings taking place in Cape Elizabeth and in the city of Portland.

"Try not to get nervous," she said, "but we're going to send you up in the helicopter with Jack Peterson from CNN."

My head drew back with shock. "What? Why *me*?"

Gary broke in. "Because you're the most knowledgeable structures specialist we have, and you're charming and well spoken."

I scoffed. "But I'm not a spokesperson," I reminded them. "And I've never been on TV before."

"Don't worry, he's not going to film you," Carol said. "He'll be filming the crash site from the air. But he's been incredibly helpful to us today, and we want to make sure he's getting the correct information because there's a lot of speculation out there right now, and everyone's following his lead."

"But I don't know what the correct information is yet," I told her. "That's the most important part of my job—*not* to form any conclusions until we have all the evidence. You know what I mean? And we've only just started to gather information."

She pointed her finger at me. "Yes. That is *exactly* what we want you to convey—that we need time to do this investigation properly, and we need the public to be patient, which isn't always easy."

"Especially for the victims' families," I added, quietly.

"That's right," she replied, nodding her head. "And you're always incredibly respectful of that, Meg. That's why we value you so much. It's why you've risen so quickly to become a senior specialist. You're brilliant, you're intuitive, and you're always tremendously sensitive."

"Thank you," I replied, lowering my gaze, because I wasn't in this for the compliments, or to rise in the NTSB hierarchy. I just wanted to do a good job, prevent more accidents from happening, and provide some closure to the families—if that was even possible.

Just the thought of the victims' families in that moment, and what they must be going through, weighed heavily on my mind. I looked out the window again at the passing landscape and let out a sigh, struggling to regroup emotionally.

Heaven help me. This was only the first day.

I pondered the fact that I had once thought this job would get easier over time, that I would somehow become immune to the emotional side of it, but that wasn't the case at all. My anxiety only seemed to be getting worse with every crash.

Of course, I didn't tell Gary that.

"Is there anything I *shouldn't* say?" I asked Carol. "Or anything in particular you want me to communicate?"

"Just that we're doing everything we can to find answers and to provide the FBI with whatever information and expertise they need from us."

Our driver turned left at the sign for Crescent Beach. As we drove down the lane and approached the main parking lot, my heart began to race, but not in the usual way. This was something different. It wasn't dread or distress. It was plain old-fashioned nervousness, because I was about to meet someone very famous.

I saw the news helicopter waiting. It was surrounded by more news trucks and a few cop cars with flashing lights. We had to stop at a barricade to speak to an armed military guard who waved us through.

A few seconds later, we pulled to a halt. Gary and Carol got out, and I quickly gathered up my things to follow.

CHAPTER

Twenty–one

It wasn't like me to get flustered at a time like this, because I'd met more than my share of reporters since I started at the Safety Board. Big or small, plane crashes always attracted a news crew. But this wasn't just any reporter I was about to meet. It was the very famous Jack Peterson.

With butterflies swarming in my belly, I hurried to catch up with Gary and Carol, who were walking briskly toward the CNN truck. I found myself deliberating over ridiculous things like…should I get rid of the ponytail?

No, I should keep it for the helicopter ride, because I'd be wearing a headset.

Should I mention that I had watched and followed his recovery on television and admired his courage and fortitude?

No, Meg. People probably said that to him all the time. No doubt, he was sick of hearing it.

Don't be a fan girl. You're just here to do your job.

The passenger side door of the news truck opened, and I felt a strange rush of anticipation as Mr. Peterson got out.

Dressed in loose-fitting jeans and a light blue shirt under a navy crew-neck sweater, he wasn't as tall as I'd imagined. But that didn't make him any less striking. He was very fit and muscular—and better looking than any man had a right to be.

Still feeling nervous, I watched intently as Mr. Peterson moved to greet Carol, who he'd obviously met before. He also shook Gary's hand. Then they all turned to look at me as I approached with my heavy gear bag slung over my shoulder.

Carol gestured toward me. "Jack, this is Meg Andrews, our senior structures specialist. This lady is the best. She really knows her stuff. Meg, this is Jack Peterson."

As soon as we made eye contact, the butterflies in my belly quadrupled. Up close and in person, he was even more handsome than he was on television—if that were even possible. The blueness of his eyes practically knocked the wind out of me.

I did notice, however, that he looked extremely tired and was in need of a shave. I also noticed a few small scars on his face that didn't show up on the TV screen. Hidden under makeup, no doubt.

Fighting to push the butterflies down, I reached out to shake his hand.

"Hi, Meg," he said. "Thanks so much for coming up with me today. I know how busy you must be. I really appreciate it."

"It's no problem," I replied. "It's an honor. Really."

Oh God. Was that too much?

He gestured toward the helicopter. The pilot was already in his seat and the door was wide open, waiting for us.

"Ready to go?" Jack asked.

"Yes." I gave Gary a quick look of disbelief as I passed him and followed the superstar newsman to the chopper.

~*C*

"At least the rain has held off," Jack said as we buckled in.

We sat beside each other in the rear passenger cabin while we waited for another CNN reporter to join us. We hadn't put on our headsets yet.

I took a moment to look around at all the video equipment and monitors, the overwhelming array of buttons, knobs and gauges, while Jack adjusted the laptop console that operated the exterior camera. I had noticed it when I got in. It was housed in a nose-mounted gimbal out front, and could rotate 360 degrees.

"We'll get some good footage with this machine," he said, referring to the chopper in general.

"Will you be broadcasting live?"

"No," he replied, "but we'll be able to transmit the footage to the station right away."

I craned my neck to look up at the sky. "I sure hope the rain continues to hold off."

I knew that I didn't have to explain anything to this man about how much more difficult the rescue and recovery would be if the weather turned. He'd seen and covered his own share of disasters of all kinds. He most certainly knew it.

"Listen…" I said, turning to him. "Thanks for that video you shot last night, and for sharing it with us. It's going to be very helpful."

"Of course," he replied.

"It must have been terrifying," I went on, "to have seen all that, right in front of your own home."

"It was." He inhaled deeply. "I'm still pretty shaken up by it, to be honest. I've seen a lot of things in my career, but that…" He gazed at me for a few seconds, seeming unable to find the right words to continue, and I nodded with understanding.

"And it's my parents' house, not mine," he added, looking away, in an obvious effort to change the subject.

"Have they lived there all their lives?"

"Sort of. It's a summer place. They still have their home base in Chicago where I grew up and went to school."

"I see."

I paused, watching his profile for a few seconds while he flipped a few switches on the video control panel. I couldn't help but marvel at his looks. Strong jawline, nice lips and a perfect nose. *God*, he was unbelievably attractive. Impossible not to stare at. I wondered how old he was. Early forties, maybe?

I could probably google that, along with all sorts of other personal information about him if I wanted to—like whether or not he was married.

I glanced at his hand. He wasn't wearing a ring.

Not that I wanted to date him or anything. I was already in a long-term relationship.

With Malcolm.

But even if I wasn't, I was too busy to date. Too focused on my job. I was simply—for some reason I couldn't explain—curious about Jack's personal life, like some kind of voyeur. Maybe I wondered what it would be like to be him, so rich and famous.

"Which house do your parents own, if you don't mind me asking?" I had to get my mind back on track, remember the investigation. "It would help us to know exactly where the camera was filming from, to determine angles, trajectory…"

"It's the blue one right behind the Kettle Cove Parking Lot," he replied. "We'll fly over it in a few minutes. I'll show you."

"That would be great. Thank you."

We sat in silence for a moment, waiting, and I had to work hard not to keep staring at him, which wasn't easy. He was like some sort of human magnet for my eyes.

"Do you know anything about the arrival of the families?" I asked.

It was common practice for the airline to fly victims' families to the crash location and put them up in a hotel somewhere nearby. Once they arrived, members of our team and other authorities would meet with them for daily briefings—which was never easy.

"A few are already here," Jack said. "The rest are on their way." He shook his head. "It's going to be difficult for them over the next few weeks, and beyond."

"Yes."

His eyes turned to me, and I felt like a deer caught in headlights as he studied my expression intently.

Then he leaned forward to peer out the door, probably looking for the other reporter, who still hadn't arrived. Jack sat back in his seat. "Mind if I ask how you came into this job?"

I shifted slightly in the seat. "It may seem a bit strange to you."

"Now I'm intrigued."

Something stirred in my veins. Maybe it was the way he was looking at me with those penetrating blue eyes.

I suddenly found myself struggling to keep a cool head

when my entire body was responding to the nearness of him. It was as if there were some kind of electric current in the chopper, buzzing all around us. I'd never felt anything quite like it before. But then again, I'd never met anyone so famous.

Clearing my throat, I tried to get my thoughts in order to form a proper reply. "Well…" I cleared throat again. "I grew up with a terrible fear of flying, from a very young age. I don't know why. By the time I reached college, I had no choice but to fly back and forth across the country if I wanted to see my boyfriend, who was in medical school at the time. He was in California while I was at Princeton."

"What did you study there?" Jack asked.

"Structural engineering," I told him, "but even then, I didn't know this was where I would end up. I thought I'd be building skyscrapers or something. Sometimes I thought I might become an architect and build houses. That was my intention, originally, when I was younger, but then I got sidetracked by aviation.

"Anyhow, my brother happened to be a pilot, and he took me up in a private plane one summer to try and get me over my phobia. Oddly enough, it worked—*eventually*—and I ended up becoming a pilot myself. Pure stubbornness, I guess, to conquer that fear. Anyway, in my last year at Princeton, I got a summer job at the Safety Board, and that was that. I was hooked and I knew this was what I needed to do with my life."

Jack nodded. "What happened to the boyfriend?"

I laughed nervously. "We're still together, though we live in different cities. We don't see each other all that often, but it works because we're both addicted to our jobs and we work a lot of hours. He's a surgeon now, and I do a lot of traveling."

Jack was still watching me with interest, and I felt an inexplicable urge to explain further, even though I knew I was starting to ramble.

I waved my hand through the air. "A situation like this could mean we're away from home, living in hotels for weeks at a time, maybe months. Even when I'm back in the office, I practically eat, live and breathe whatever investigation I'm working on. I'm kind of obsessed." I paused. "But Malcolm's the same way, putting in a lot of hours at the hospital, and I always knew he would never leave the West Coast."

Jack stared at me with a furrowed brow, inclining his head slightly, as if he were still trying to figure me out.

Was he like this with everyone? I wondered. Maybe that's why he was such a good interviewer. He had a curious mind.

I saw the other reporter jump out of the back of the news truck just then, and shut the doors. He stood for a moment, checking his phone, still keeping us waiting.

"It's weird," Jack said, staring intently at me. "I know we've never met before, but there's something very familiar about you. I can't put my finger on it." His gaze roamed over my face, and he seemed to be hoping I would have something to say about that.

"Oh…" Unfortunately, I was speechless.

I couldn't deny I felt strangely flattered by his interest in me.

"You're familiar to me as well," I finally said. "But I think you're familiar to most people in America."

He nodded, and gazed off in the direction of the crash site across the water. "Maybe we knew each other in a former life."

I chuckled. "Yeah, maybe."

The other reporter climbed into the chopper just then. "Sorry about that." He took a seat next to the pilot in the forward cabin. "I was just reading my texts. They found one of the wings in the ocean."

"Excellent," I said. "What about the tail or the black box?"

"I don't know about that," he said. "They didn't mention it." He turned around and shook my hand. "Hi, I'm Joe."

"I'm Meg. I'm with the National Transportation Safety Board."

"I know," he replied. Then he spoke to Jack. "I told the crew at the lighthouse that we'd get some aerial footage of them bringing it up. It's quite a ways out, apparently. And they're still working on collecting the rest of the floating debris."

"They'll be working on that for a while," I said, knowing there must be body parts as well. But I chose not to mention that.

Someone outside the chopper shut the doors for us, and I put on my headset.

"Will you be analyzing the data from the black box when they find it?" Jack asked me.

"No, we have different specialists for that," I explained. "They'll take it back to Washington and look at it there, along with the cockpit voice recorder. And of course, the FBI will be involved."

"Because it might have been a bomb," Jack said, studying my face.

"We don't know that yet," I said firmly. "It's far too early to form any conclusions. Explosions can be caused by all sorts of things, so it's very important that we examine every inch of the wreckage and explore all possibilities in order to determine the true cause. It's crucial that we don't make premature assumptions that might lead us or the public down the wrong path."

Jack nodded. "Okay," he said firmly. "I get what you're saying."

That was easy, I thought.

The pilot started the chopper engine, and it was very noisy beneath the spinning rotors. I had to speak to Jack through the headset.

"We're going to need some time to put all the puzzle pieces together," I added. "We can't rush it."

He was listening to me carefully. I felt that he was reading my expression through my eyes, listening to the nuances in my voice, even though he could only hear me through the wire.

The helicopter lifted off the ground just then, and I jumped at the sensation.

Jack touched my arm and regarded me with concern. "Are you okay?"

I nodded, embarrassed. "Yes. I'm fine. I just wasn't expecting it right at that second." I had come to realize a long time ago that although I had "conquered" my fear of flying, I hadn't actually gotten rid of it. I'd simply taught myself how to cope. "And I guess I'm a bit jittery today. The first day at a crash site is always…" How to put it? "*Difficult.*"

We rose into the air, flew over the sandy beach and across the water toward the crash site, where I had been working near Jack's parents' house.

He leaned over me to point out the window. "It's the blue one, right down there."

I turned my head to look at him. His face was very close to mine, mere inches away, and I was extremely aware of his nearness…the stubble on his jaw, his thick, dark, wavy hair, and the way he smelled—like very expensive men's musk. Everything about him affected me physically, which was strange, because I wasn't single, nor was I interested in flirtations of any kind. I was perfectly content with Malcolm and passionate about my work.

I swallowed hard to try and get my wits together.

Forcing myself to turn my attention back to the window, I studied the crash site from the sky and searched the surrounding area for other missing pieces of debris that needed to be recovered. I was still hoping we would find the other wing, and of course, the tail and black box.

"I don't know about you," Jack said, "but seeing something like this always makes me want to go straight home and hug my loved ones."

"Me, too," I said with melancholy, briefly meeting his gaze.

Then we both set to work, focusing on the task of taking photographs from the sky and searching the surrounding area for more wreckage. Jack had plenty of questions for me along the way, but he was fairly knowledgeable already, having covered airline disasters before.

He was an incredibly intelligent and fascinating man.

⌒

An hour later, back at the Crescent Beach parking lot, the helicopter touched down. I checked the time. It was nearly 3:00 p.m. and I wanted some more time at the crash site before our team meeting at 6:00 p.m. at the hotel in Portland where we had set up our command headquarters.

Following that, there would be a debriefing for the families, followed by a press conference an hour later. All of this would take place in the ballroom of the hotel. The FBI would be the lead agency, but we needed to be present as well.

The pilot shut off the engine, and the noise of the rotors died down. Jack checked his phone while I removed my headset.

When he finished reading his messages, he removed his headset as well. "Are you heading straight back to the crash site now?" he asked.

"Yes. I still have a lot of work to do over there." I gathered up my gear bag and waited for Jack to open the chopper door.

"Would you mind if I shadowed you for a bit this afternoon?" he asked. "I'd like to see what you do, get a feel for how you approach things, so I can talk about that on my show tonight. I promise I won't get in your way."

I swallowed uneasily. "I'm afraid that part of the crash site is restricted for the press at the moment. I'd have to ask Carol, and she'd probably have to clear it with the FBI."

Jack gave me a look that struck me as slightly apologetic. "Actually, I already asked her." He held up his phone. "I hope you don't mind, but she was able to clear it for me. As long as I don't bring in a camera crew, or start broadcasting from there, she said it would be fine. I'm not due back on the air until later tonight anyway, after the press conference. Just between you and me, I'm supposed to be sleeping right now."

"Ah. I've been up all night, too," I told him.

"Running on pure adrenaline, I expect."

"Yes."

Someone outside the chopper opened the door and I started to get out.

"When will you be able to take a break?" Jack asked, hopping down behind me.

"I'll sleep for a few hours after dark," I replied. "I don't want to waste any daylight hours."

He waved at a black car that was parked on the opposite side of the lot, waiting for us, apparently.

"You're very dedicated," Jack said as it drove toward us.

"So are you."

Joe was the last to exit the chopper. As he walked past us to return to the news truck, he tapped Jack on the shoulder. "I'll see you at the hotel."

"Yeah." The car pulled up and Jack opened the door for me. "After you."

I climbed into the back seat, and he slid in beside me. It was a luxurious vehicle with leather upholstery and a driver who wore a black blazer, shirt and tie.

Again, I was intensely aware of Jack's physical presence, but most especially the way he watched me, as if he were equally fascinated. I wasn't sure if I was imagining it—because he was so famous and charismatic—or if there truly was a spark between us. A chemistry like I'd never felt before. Not even with Kyle or Malcolm. And it wasn't just physical attraction. It was something else. Something a bit more mysterious. It was almost like…

It was as if I recognized him and he recognized me, but neither of us could place the other.

Or maybe I was just starstruck.

Sleep deprived.

Imagining things.

The driver took us out of the parking lot and back to the main crash site, where we spent the next few hours combing through debris. Jack was at my side the entire time, asking smart questions about what I was learning when I kicked over a certain piece of metal or examined the charred fabric on an airline seat.

The whole situation was unusual. During my career thus far, I'd answered hundreds of reporters' questions and I was always extremely careful not to say things that might lead them to speculate about what conclusions I was forming in my mind—because I was never forming any conclusions at this stage.

But with Jack, I trusted him to understand. I admired his patience, and I found myself letting down my guard. With total trust. For some reason I couldn't quite fathom, I was confident that he wouldn't disappoint me.

I was just packing up my gear to hitch a ride to the hotel with Jack when my cell phone rang. I pulled it out of my pocket and checked the call display.

I glanced at Jack, who stood waiting, flipping through his own messages.

"It's my brother," I said. "I should take this."

"No problem," Jack replied. "I'll wait for you at the car. Take your time."

He strode across the debris field toward the parking lot, and I swiped the screen on my phone. "Hello?"

"Hey, sis," Wayne said. "How are you doing out there?"

I glanced around at the giant burned-out wreck of a 747 beside me, the plethora of FBI workers, cops, and emergency vehicles, and was grateful to hear the calm sound of my brother's loving voice.

"Well, you know how it is. It's not exactly a happy place to be."

He was quiet for a moment. "Are you taking care of yourself, Meg?"

"I'm trying," I replied.

"Did you eat anything today?" He knew me too well, this big brother of mine, always looking out for me.

"I had a muffin on the flight, and one of the guys went out to get us some sandwiches awhile ago. But you know me. It's kind of hard to eat on the first day."

Wayne spoke with compassion. "I know, kid. Just make sure you get something in you, okay? And get some sleep. You can't save the world from another plane crash in one day, and you certainly can't do it if you end up back in the ER."

I didn't enjoy being reminded of that embarrassing incident. "That was nothing," I said. "And it was a year ago."

He scoffed into the phone. "You had chest pains, Meg. That's not nothing."

Holding the phone to my ear with my shoulder, I zipped up my gear bag. "It was just a bit of anxiety and they didn't even admit me," I argued. "It's not like I was having a heart attack or anything."

"But you thought you were. You gave me the fright of my life, and there was nothing I could do because you were halfway across the country, in a remote location on a mountain."

I picked up my bag and started walking toward Jack's car. "I know, I'm sorry, but I'm fine now, and I had a sandwich today, so you can relax. And I'm leaving the crash site now and heading to the hotel." I paused, for effect. "With Jack Peterson, if you must know. In his car with his own personal driver. I've been with him for most of the day."

There was a shocked silence on the other end of the line. "*The* Jack Peterson?"

"Yeah. Have you been watching CNN?"

"Of course," Wayne replied. "Who hasn't? Are you going to be on TV?"

I glanced toward the parking lot, where Jack was also talking on his cell phone, strolling around in small circles. "I don't think so. He hasn't been filming me. He just wants to learn so that he'll have good information for his show tonight."

Wayne was quiet for a few seconds. "So what's he like in real life?"

I continued to watch Jack from a distance as I walked. "He's very nice. Surprisingly down-to-earth. Very intelligent and genuine." I chose not to mention the fact that he was also incredibly attractive and a terrible distraction.

"I'm glad to hear that," Wayne said. "I'd be disappointed if it was all an act."

"It's not," I assured him. "So how are you doing in the wake of all this? Are you flying today?"

"Yeah. Pretty soon, actually, and we were just told that we'll be shuttling some of the family members to New York for a connection to Portland. They didn't want to fly with Jaeger-Woodrow Airways."

I looked down at my feet. "I can't blame them. Be safe, okay?"

"Always," Wayne replied. "And don't worry about me, sis. You know what they say."

"Safer than driving." I stepped onto the pavement and approached Jack's car. "I gotta go now. I'll talk to you later."

I met Jack's gaze. He quickly finished his own call and slipped his phone into his pocket.

"Ready?" he asked as I reached him.

"Ready as ever." He opened the car door for me, and I slid into the back seat where he joined me.

"Thanks for waiting," I said, as we buckled our seatbelts.

"No problem. Was that the brother you mentioned was a pilot?"

"Yes. His name is Wayne. He was just calling to make sure I was doing okay."

The driver started up the car and pulled out of the lot.

"I take it you and he are close?" Jack asked.

"Very. I can't imagine life without him. Although he does give me a hard time, occasionally."

"About what?" Jack asked with interest.

Maybe I shouldn't have felt so comfortable with a CNN reporter, but all my filters seemed to fall away whenever he asked me a question.

"Oh," I said dismissively, "he just thinks I work too hard. But he's probably right. I do. He's always after me to take time off and get away from it all."

Again, Jack simply watched my face, seeming fascinated by every word I spoke. I couldn't help but start to ramble again.

"I guess I am a *bit* of a workaholic. But it's not just work to me. It's my passion." I turned slightly on the seat to face him more directly. "You must work a lot too. Especially when you're on location, covering something like this."

"For sure," he said with a nod. "Sometimes I think the same thing—that I'm a workaholic—because I rarely feel the need to take a vacation. It makes me think of that saying…if you love what you do, you'll never work a day in your life."

I thought about that. "Hmm. I believe that's true for most people, but for me… I can't really say that I *love* what I do. Of course, I'm very passionate about it and driven to get the job done—and done *well*—but it's hard to love the hours you spend in a place where people have died. And it's not fun to explain to families the details about why their loved ones aren't with them anymore. It's stressful and painful, and sometimes I wish my passion were something different, because there's a price to pay."

"What price?"

I shrugged. "Besides the stress and anxiety on a crash site, which can be overwhelming sometimes, I don't have a normal life. I'm too busy. I can't imagine how I could ever be a mother in this line of work, because it's all-consuming. Which is kind of disappointing, in a way, now that I think about it. I always imagined I'd get married someday and have kids. Now suddenly, I'm thirty. How did that happen? But *God*, I don't have time to date anyone."

"I thought you said you were still with your boyfriend from college. What was his name?"

"Malcolm," I quickly replied. "And yes, I'm with him, but it's not a new relationship, so it doesn't require that we *date*. Not after nine years. You know how that is… It's just…easy and comfortable."

I gazed out the window at the trees as we increased speed on the main road to Portland, and realized my life must sound kind of pathetic. I kept saying how passionate I was about my work, *but personally*? I was describing my boyfriend like he was an old shoe. And I kept saying the word "date" like it was something I was allergic to.

I turned my attention back to Jack, who was still watching me.

"My brother's always after me to find balance," I added. "He tells me to go to a movie or take a dance class. He's right, of course. I do need to get out and do other things, because the way I live… It just isn't healthy."

I stopped talking, and Jack and I simply stared at each other. He was nodding his head.

I felt self-conscious all of a sudden. "I can't believe I just said all that to you. I'm so sorry."

Jack's eyebrows lifted. "Don't apologize. I get it, totally. I'm the same way. I can be obsessed with my job, too. Although I do take vacations, and I was very insistent about getting seven weeks a year written into my most recent contract."

"Seven weeks. Wow, that's great. What do you do with all that time?"

He smiled at me, and I felt a rush of warmth spread through my body. "I travel, I come here and spend time with my parents. I lie on beaches, go skiing, sailing, hiking, sightseeing. With no cameras or interviews required."

I smiled, and realized it was the first time I had smiled since my arrival in Maine. "I should take notes."

"Yes, young lady, you definitely should," he said. "I can put it in an email for you later, if you like."

I chuckled. "No, I think I got it. So who do you go on all these adventure vacations with? Do you have a girlfriend?"

Seriously, Meg? Filters!

I pressed my open hand to my mouth. "I'm sorry again. That's none of my business."

The corner of Jack's lips curled into a small grin which I found incredibly sexy. It was exciting and invigorating, and all the little hairs on my arms and neck started to rise and tingle.

Be careful, Meg. You're not here for this.
But what was this, exactly? What was happening here?

Clearly, Jack found me entertaining. "It's fine," he said

with a small chuckle. "And no, I don't have a girlfriend, but not for lack of trying."

I gave him a look. "Oh, please. You're Jack Peterson. You must have beautiful women propositioning you all the time."

His expression was friendly and open as he shrugged slightly. "I've never been terribly interested in the kinds of women who proposition me. Not these days. Or maybe I've just given up on romance. Too many disappointments."

"I hear you on that count. I've never had much luck in the romance department either."

"Says the woman who's been in a relationship for nine years."

I bit my lower lip and regarded him with a hint of chagrin. "That was an odd thing for me to say, wasn't it?"

He shrugged again. "I'm not judging."

I realized in that moment that I still hadn't talked to Malcolm since I'd left the message on his phone the night before, and he hadn't called me either. Of course, he knew how busy I would be today, and he always respected the space I needed in order to do my job. He was probably just waiting for me to call him when I had a free moment. Or maybe he was in the OR.

Jack and I drove on in silence for a while as I pondered my relationship with Malcolm. Had it really been nine years? It was hard to believe.

I turned to Jack again. "How long will you stay in Maine for all this? Or will you head back to New York right away?"

"I don't know yet," he replied. "We'll be taking it day by day, but I suspect I'll be here the whole week. What about you?"

"It's really hard to say. It depends what we find in the next few days. If we end up having to reconstruct the plane, it could be a long time."

He considered that. "Well, if you need some downtime this week, give me a call. We could get a drink or something."

Was Jack Peterson asking me out?

No…he knew I was in a relationship. He probably just wanted to stay informed about the crash.

"That would be nice," I replied. "But I always work until pretty late."

"So do I. Here. Take my number. Text me at any hour. I might be up."

"Okay." I pulled out my cell phone and he told me his number. I added it to my list of contacts, which felt very surreal, to have Jack Peterson's personal cell phone number in my phone.

I gave him my number as well.

His driver slowed at the entrance to the hotel parking lot where dozens of satellite news trucks—including one from CNN—were parked along the road. By now, news teams had arrived from all over the world—France, Germany, Australia, and other places. Crowds of photographers with cameras stood behind a barricade, and cops and paddy wagons with flashing lights created a very intense atmosphere.

"Looks like it's going to be a packed house," Jack said.

He lowered the window to speak to a police officer in a bright yellow vest who stood on the street, directing traffic. Jack held up his press badge. "I'm here for the debriefing, and this lady is with the National Transportation Safety Board. She's staying in the hotel."

The cop bent at the waist to peer in at me. "How do you do, ma'am. Everything looks good here, Mr. Peterson. Go on in."

We pulled into the lot, and the driver dropped us off under the overhang at the main entrance.

"Are you coming inside now?" I asked Jack as I unbuckled my seatbelt.

"No, I'll head over to the news truck and find Joe," he said. "We still have a few hours before the press conference starts. Good luck in there, okay?"

"You, too. Thanks for the drive."

"Anytime."

I got out with my heavy gear bag, shut the car door behind me, and walked into the hotel.

What a day it had been.

And it wasn't over yet. The really difficult part was only just beginning.

CHAPTER

Twenty-three

Jack

As I watched Meg Andrews disappear through the sliding glass doors of the hotel, I marveled at the fact that I might be entertaining a bit of a crush. It was a rare and unexpected thing, especially in circumstances like these, where I was focused on covering a major global disaster.

Last night, a commercial airliner had narrowly missed crashing into my parents' house—by a mere few hundred yards. We were all lucky to be alive, and today, not a moment had passed where I didn't think about that.

Or the poor dead child and the battered teddy bear I had seen in the darkness late last night.

The memory caused a knot in my stomach and a heaviness in my chest. No doubt, the images would be burned into my consciousness for the rest of my life, and beyond.

For that reason, I, like everyone else in the world, wanted answers about why this tragedy occurred, and I wanted assurances that it would never happen again. Maybe that was an impossible dream, but I wanted it, all the same.

So did Meg Andrews. She struck me as an exceedingly competent professional who was deeply and passionately motivated to determine the cause of an accident, and make recommendations for improvements to safety and security. With people like her at work on the investigation, I believed we were in good hands.

But there was something else about her that caused a curious spark of interest in me—something outside the fact that I found her mind-bogglingly attractive, even in those unflattering black trousers, black work boots and bulky NTSB jacket.

Meg wore no makeup. Her blond hair was tied back in an untidy ponytail, but that worked for me, because I had never been into the glamorous types. I'd lost interest in women like that at a very young age.

Consequently, I hadn't been able to take my eyes off Meg for most of the afternoon. There was something about her that struck a chord in me the instant she got out of the car and walked toward me, across the parking lot. I'd felt it even before we spoke a word to each other.

Some people might call it love at first sight, but I knew it wasn't as simple or romantic as that. It was a deeper, more longstanding recognition. Though I had no idea who Meg might have been to me in another life and time, I knew she was *someone*. And this was significant, because I'd never felt this way about anyone in my current life except for Katelyn, which was why I had once believed she was the only one for me.

It turned out that she wasn't. She had been the one for my brother.

All that aside, this feeling I had about Meg was not the same. With Katelyn, I had conscious, vivid memories of our past together, even before I met her. With Meg, there was only an intuitive sense of familiarity and connection. I wondered if I would *ever* know who she was, with certainty.

"Let's get going," I said to Curtis, my driver. He took me out of the hotel parking lot to where Joe waited for me in the news truck, half a block away.

My cell phone rang just then, and I checked the call display. What a coincidence.

"Katelyn," I said, answering the call. I checked my wristwatch. "You must be getting ready to go on the air."

"Yes," she said, "in about ten minutes. I just wanted to check in with you. I'm assuming you'll be at the press conference tonight?"

"Yeah, I'm here at the hotel right now. I'll attend the briefing, then I'll do my show immediately afterwards. We'll do it live from the Portland Head Light."

"That's a good spot," she said. "I'll be at the briefing as well, as soon as I finish up here, so I'll probably see you there."

"I'll keep an eye out for you," I replied.

"Okay. See you later."

I ended the call and got out of the car.

~*e*

Not surprisingly, the press conference was intense.

I sat in the front row, listening to the local authorities describe the crash and rescue effort. All the while, I was aware of Meg, who sat at the end of a long table of experts with Gary and Carol. She looked pasty white, almost green, and she kept her gaze lowered as the navy explained that they would not yet call off the search for survivors in the water, even though no one had yet been found alive. The subtext was, of course, that we should all prepare ourselves for a very high death toll and no survivors.

Other reports were equally grim. We learned that a local community center had been converted into a temporary morgue for the bodies that had been recovered so far. The medical examiner was as delicate and tactful as he could possibly be, as he described the extent of the casualties.

There was a mad flurry of questions when the FBI spokesperson delivered his report. Unfortunately, none of the authorities had any concrete or new information about whether or not it had been an act of terrorism, or some sort of mechanical failure on the plane.

He was unable to relay any information about the black box, which had not yet been found, and the weather was turning. They expected rain and high winds that night.

One thing was certain. There had been a massive explosion in the air. Witnesses on the ground had described it as a sudden fireball, accompanied by a thunderous noise that was heard all over Cape Elizabeth and as far as Portland and even Augusta.

Based on what the authorities now knew about the crash and the wreckage on land and in the water, it was clear that the explosion had occurred toward the center of the aircraft, causing it to break in half. Most of the front half landed near my home, while the rear of the plane had been blown to bits. This was what made the recovery so difficult in the water off Cape Elizabeth. It was a debris field full of small pieces, long-sunk or floating with the current.

Lastly, a representative from the airline stood up to offer his regrets and condolences to the families. He promised to fully support the investigation, help in every possible way, and provide any and all information that the authorities required.

A few family members stood up to shout at him and ask angry questions about airline security. The press conference had to be cut short.

As soon as they shut down the briefing, I noticed Meg—who had not been required to speak—get up from her chair and hurry out the back door of the ballroom.

Though I was expected back at the news truck to go live on the air in thirty minutes, I pushed through the noisy crowd to follow her.

CHAPTER

Twenty-four

"I'm embarrassed that you're seeing me like this," Meg said, bending over with her hands braced on her knees. She had just vomited into a trash can.

I handed her my bottle of water. She unscrewed the cap and took a sip, then wiped her watery eyes with the back of her hand.

"I don't know what's wrong with me," she said. "I've done hundreds of briefings over the past decade, and I've seen and heard a lot of stuff, but I've never reacted like this. Maybe it was something I ate."

People walked by, gaping at us curiously. Sometimes it sucked to be a celebrity.

"Don't be embarrassed," I said in a low voice as I took hold of her arm and guided her to an alcove in a less busy corridor. "It was rough in there."

She nodded her head and leaned against the wall. "Maybe I should think about retiring. I can't seem to handle this like I used to."

She closed her eyes and shook her head with frustration, then stared at me directly. I was momentarily overcome by the depth of feeling in those beautiful eyes.

"You've seen a lot too," she said. "I know you have…over in Afghanistan. And this isn't your first airline disaster."

"Unfortunately I've covered a few."

"And the bomb that you survived…" she continued, "and all your injuries. The pain. You lost your friends. I can't imagine what that must have been like."

We regarded each other steadily, while people flooded through the busier corridor, talking heatedly about the briefing. All I wanted to do was stay hidden where we were and talk to Meg some more, or take her somewhere less chaotic—away from all this—but the clock was ticking. I checked my wristwatch.

"You have to go," she said. "You have a show to do. I shouldn't be keeping you."

I didn't want to leave, but I hadn't touched base with my producer yet.

"I'm sorry," I said. "Are you going to be okay?"

"Of course. I'm feeling better now, and I have a lot to do, too. I should text Gary and see where we're supposed to be right now. He's probably looking for me." She pushed away from the wall and pulled her phone out of her pocket, then gave me a small smile. "Break a leg."

I rolled my eyes. "I already did that once. Don't really want to do it again."

She grimaced apologetically. "Poor choice of words."

I started backing away from her, still not wanting to leave. "I'll text you later to see how you're doing. After the show. Will you watch?"

"Probably not," she said. "There's so much to do tonight."

I understood. "No worries. But I'll still text you."

"Please do."

I experienced a rush of anticipation at her response, and couldn't wait to text her after my show.

What the heck was going on here? I felt like I was back in middle school, crushing on the new girl.

She turned her attention to her phone, while I took off in a run toward the news truck.

I was halfway across the empty ballroom when I spotted Katelyn, talking to the Portland mayor, who I'd interviewed earlier that morning.

Still dressed in a suit and heels, having come straight from the station with her red hair swept up in a loose bun, Katelyn noticed me and waved.

"Don't you have a show to do?" she called out from the back corner of the ballroom.

"Yeah, I'm late," I replied, without breaking my stride.

"Call me later," she said.

I nodded and continued on.

CHAPTER

Twenty-five

Meg

As it happened, I *did* watch Jack's show on CNN that night, because Gary ordered me back to my room to rest and regroup. He reminded me that I had been working non-stop for thirty hours under high-stress conditions, and that if I was going to be any good to him in the coming days, I had to get some sleep.

He was right, of course. He was always right about things like that, which was why he was the boss and I wasn't.

I followed his advice and took a shower. Then I sat down on the foot of my bed in the white terry hotel bathrobe, with my long, wet hair wrapped in a towel. I pointed the remote control at the TV and turned on CNN.

Jack's show was just starting. While I watched the opening, I pulled the towel from my hair and began to dry the ends.

I had watched his show many times in the past, but everything was different tonight because now I knew him personally. I found myself captivated by every word he spoke, every hint of emotion or reference to something we had seen together or discussed that day. Everything he relayed was accurate and spot on.

I had no regrets about allowing him to shadow me that afternoon, or about letting down my guard. In fact, I was glad. There was something about Jack Peterson that had a calming effect on me. It seemed to permeate through the television screen as he urged everyone to have patience while we sought answers.

He was also unbelievably sensitive and compassionate about the human side of this terrible catastrophe. He spent a significant amount of time highlighting the kindness, compassion and generosity of the people of Maine. He described fishermen and yachtsmen who had risen from their beds to help search the waters off Cape Elizabeth all night long. Women's groups made plates of sandwiches by the hundreds, working tirelessly and with little hope for a good outcome. Others were opening their homes to family members of the victims, or offering their cars for them to use. Stress counsellors had volunteered their services, and emergency workers had stepped up to the plate in every possible way. At times, I could barely watch through my tears.

The fact that I hadn't slept in over thirty-six hours didn't help matters. I was exhausted and emotional, and I felt the grief of the families like never before.

Inching back across the bed to rest my head against the pillows, I listened to all of Jack's interviews. He spoke about the recovery of the tail, and I saw the aerial footage we had recorded in the helicopter.

Part of me wanted to get up off the bed and go downstairs to the command headquarters right then and there, and learn the latest information about the investigation, but I resisted the urge. Gary had been clear.

He didn't want to see me until I had slept for at least six hours. He promised to brief me in the morning.

As Jack's show came to an end, I curled up in a ball on the bed, and squeezed the feather pillow under my cheek. I couldn't keep my eyes open. Within seconds, I fell into a deep slumber with the lights and television on. I didn't wake until my alarm went off at 6:00 a.m.

That's when I realized I hadn't heard my phone buzz with an incoming text, shortly after 11:00 p.m.

Are you still up?

Instantly wide awake, I sat up on the bed and replied.

~*O*

Good morning Jack. Sorry I didn't reply to your text last night. Gary ordered me back to my room to sleep. I watched your show…it was good. But then my head hit the pillow and that was it. If I don't see you today, maybe a drink tonight?

Excitement flooded my veins as I pressed send, even while I worried that I was playing with fire. I still hadn't spoken to Malcolm since I arrived in Maine, and he was probably wondering what had become of me.

Jack immediately texted back.

No worries. I was tired, too. I went back to my parents' house and slept like a log. I might see you today if you're at the crash site. My mother has been baking. She wants to do something to help. There will be cookies and coffee tomorrow for everyone within a square mile of our house.

I smiled and texted him back. *That's very sweet of her. What kind of cookies?*

He replied: *Two kinds. Oatmeal raisin and chocolate chip.*
Please tell her thank you.

He responded with a thumbs up icon, and I set my phone down to get dressed and hurry down to work.

~⊘

It was too early to call Malcolm, so I sent him a text as I was leaving my room.

Hey there. Just touching base to let you know I'm still alive. It's crazy here. Working non-stop. Give me a call when you have some time.

I pressed send, slipped my phone into my pocket, and approached the elevators.

~⊘

Malcolm called a few minutes later, not long after I arrived in the conference room for our morning meeting, which hadn't started yet. I just sat down at the boardroom table when my phone buzzed.

I rose from my chair and left the room to talk to him.

"I can't talk long," he said, after explaining that he was in his office at the hospital, about to see a patient before surgery, "but I figured I should call. You certainly have your hands full, it looks like."

"Yes. Have you been watching CNN?"

"A bit, here and there," he replied. "I was in the OR all day yesterday and until late last night. Sorry for not calling sooner, but I figured you'd be busy."

"Yeah, it's been nuts."

I was quiet for a few seconds, thinking about how I had reacted after the press conference the night before. A giant mountain of stress had built up inside of me, which had begun the moment I stepped onto the crash site that morning. Then, the briefing for the families had put me over the edge.

"I'm having a rough time with this one," I confessed to Malcolm. "It's rougher than usual. I don't know why."

"How so?" he asked.

"I don't know. It's just hitting me really hard. The pain everyone is feeling… All those deaths…"

There was nothing but silence on the other end of the line. I waited for him to reply, and when he didn't, I thought we might have been cut off.

"Hello?" I said. "Malcolm? Are you there?"

Another pause. "Hello. Jeez, yeah I'm here. Sorry, I was just reading over a file. I have a patient waiting. It's a complicated case. I should go. Call me when things calm down a bit. We'll chat then."

A part of me felt completely hollowed out by his response. He seemed so very far away, and not just in terms of the physical distance between us.

It never bothered me before—the fact that he had his own career to think about and I was not his top priority. It never bothered me because, quite frankly, he wasn't my top priority either. My job was.

In that way, we were a perfect match. That's why it worked so well between us. There was never any drama.

This morning, however, his lack of interest in what I was going through left me feeling almost devastated. That, on top of the death and despair I had witnessed over the past twenty-four hours, broke me down.

"Sure," I replied in a shaky voice that I fought to control. "We'll talk another time."

I ended the call and returned to the conference room

for our morning briefing. As soon as I sat down at the table, I realized my heart was pounding hard and my stomach was burning.

With red-hot anger.

It was directed at Malcolm, which wasn't fair. I knew that my emotions were a result of everything combined— the stress of seeing what I had seen yesterday, the lack of sleep, the families' grief and anger.

Rationally, I knew it wasn't all Malcolm's fault, but I couldn't help feeling upset over how he had ignored me on the phone. He'd seemed so distracted, as if he didn't care about what was happening here and how many lives had been lost, or how hard it was on me. Did he not understand the magnitude of this? How massive and horrific it was?

"Everything okay?" Gary asked from across the table, his brow furrowed with concern. He was good at reading people. Me, especially.

I waved a hand dismissively through the air and steadied my voice. "I'm fine. That was just Malcolm. It's no big deal."

"Trouble on the home front?" Brent asked, sitting down beside me.

Brent was a systems guy. He was married with three daughters, all under the age of ten. He often talked about them with humor and love. We worked together closely, sharing information, bouncing ideas off each other.

"I wouldn't call it the home front," I replied. "Home is right here." I pointed at the table.

The way Gary looked at me then… I didn't know how to take it. His eyes were full of sympathy.

It bothered me because suddenly I felt as if everyone thought I was a pathetic loser with no life.

Maybe I was. Maybe it was time to re-evaluate a few things.

"Let's just get to work," I said. "What did I miss last night?"

Gary opened up his laptop and began to fill me in. What he told me about Jaeger-Woodrow Airways left me reeling with shock.

Meg

"Jaeger-Woodrow Airways is actually Marquee-Goldman Airlines? Are you sure?"

Marquee-Goldman had been a discount airline that went bankrupt in the early 1990s after a string of accidents related to poor safety standards, where there had been a blatant disregard for the rules of the FAA. As far as we all knew, the fleet had been broken up, and the individual jets sold off to other airlines throughout the world to pay off Marquee-Goldman's fines and creditors, who got about ten cents on the dollar.

"How could that happen?" I asked. "Weren't they fined exorbitant fees, and didn't one of the executives go to jail for something else...tax evasion related to the airline?"

"That's right," Gary said, "but it was just a slap on the wrist. Reginald Harrison was his name, and he's been running a bunch of other businesses ever since. He paid it off and barely served any time. The FBI just let us know that when he broke up Marquee-Goldman and sold the planes at a discount to smaller airlines in Europe, those airlines were owned by an umbrella corporation that he also controlled. The process is called creating a corporate veil, and it's complicated."

I sat forward. "So how does this affect our investigation? It doesn't change the fact that we still need to know what happened on this flight, and why there was an explosion at 30,000 feet."

"Absolutely," Gary said, "and for all we know, it could have been a terrorist's bomb, although no groups have come forward to take credit for it. So we're no further ahead in what we know about the accident. But we will be taking a very close look at Jaeger-Woodrow's safety procedures. Our Human Factors team at the airport is digging deep and hard on that as we speak."

"The poor families," I said, shaking my head. "To think that someone like that, a man responsible for crashes before, and forced out of the airline business, was free to start up another one. With the same planes he always owned. And because of the bankruptcy, he even got out of paying the airline's debts. Does the press know anything about this yet?"

"Not yet," Gary replied. "The FBI will be revealing it later this morning, at another briefing. But from what I understand, there's no crime on Harrison's part, in terms of the corporate shenanigans. Unless he's committing tax evasion again, he hasn't broken any laws."

"That sucks," Brent said. "My God, was he the airline representative at the briefing yesterday?"

I remembered the young man from Jaeger-Woodrow who had stood up to speak. He had seemed genuinely saddened and remorseful.

"No," Gary replied. "That was just a PR guy, and he's going to have his work cut out for him today when this news hits the fan. I actually feel sorry for him, because I suspect Harrison is lying on a beach somewhere in the South Pacific. He's rich as Croesus. Owns buildings and sports teams and all sorts of other high-profile corporations."

"That *really* sucks," Brent said.

"Yes, it does," Gary replied. "But we can't do much about his extravagant lifestyle, so let's just focus on our jobs. We need to keep looking at the wreckage, investigating what happened at the airport before the plane took off, and find that black box." He hit a few buttons on his laptop keyboard, then closed it. "So let's get to work."

~ ⊘

After I left the command headquarters with my structures team, I stepped onto the hotel elevator and immediately sent a text to Jack.

Make sure you're at the press conference later this morning. The FBI has new information. Sorry I can't say more than that, but it's not my place. I don't want to get into trouble. Just make sure you're there.

He texted me back immediately: *Thanks for the heads up. Will you be there?*

I replied: *No, I'll be at a hangar at the airport, heading up the arrival of the wreckage. Everything that's been recovered from the water so far is on its way there.*

He texted me back. *I know. We're filming it. They just loaded the wing onto a flatbed.*

I found myself smiling at my phone. *I'll probably see you sometime today then?*

Most likely, he replied.

The elevator dinged and the doors opened. I stepped off and crossed the lobby with my team to head to the airport. Our goal: to figure out exactly where the explosion had originated. I suspected I'd be doing some detailed structural reconstruction over the coming days and weeks. I hoped it would provide some answers.

Twenty-seven

Jack

"**H**ow are the kids taking all this?" I asked Katelyn, as we stood in the crowded hotel lobby with our coffees, waiting to be let into the ballroom for the morning press conference. Today, Katelyn was dressed casually in jeans and a fitted blazer, her red hair hanging loose about her shoulders.

"Ah, you know, they're kids. They've had some questions, but they're too young. They don't really understand. They just know that they can't go to Grammy's for a while because a plane has crashed next to their house, and we have to wait for it to be cleaned up. Thank God for *Dora the Explorer.*"

I nodded with understanding. "Best to keep them away. It's like a battlefield out the back window."

Katelyn sipped her coffee. "We should count ourselves lucky. Every day is a gift."

An older woman near the front of the lobby began to weep inconsolably. Her husband pulled her into his arms. Katelyn and I watched in somber silence as she was led away, onto an elevator.

"Have you spoken to Aaron since the night of the crash?" Katelyn carefully asked me.

"No, I've been busy," I explained.

"He's been busy, too," she informed me, giving me that look—the one that said she knew better than anyone how our relationship was still strained after all these years, even though we put on friendly faces in front of our families and made an effort to keep things civil.

"Busy doing what?" I asked with a hint of disinterest, imagining that Aaron was probably dealing with a critical emergency at the boat factory. Maybe the paint color was wrong on one of his new racing schooners and the billionaire who had commissioned it was in a huff.

Katelyn turned to me with disbelief. "You *do* know that he's been out on the water every hour since the crash, helping with the recovery. He's loaned a bunch of his boats and he hasn't slept a wink in two days."

Aaron?

Feeling suddenly ashamed of my assumptions, I replied, "Sorry. I didn't know that."

"Of course you didn't know. Because you don't talk to him. You're too busy being the world's best reporter, telling us all about the kindness of strangers and how that has been the one bright light in all of this—how everyone has come together in our community. I watched your show, Jack, and I saw how moved you were by it. But keep in mind—one of those kind strangers is your brother. He's out there doing a good thing, and it hasn't been easy on him."

She turned to look the other way, obviously angry with me.

"Sorry," I said again. "I'm just reporting what I see."

She faced me again. "I know, but that's the problem. You

never *see* Aaron. You don't want to see what's good in him, because you've always been in competition with him, and you hate when he wins at anything. I just wish you could realize that you've finally beaten him in the race—the race that seems to matter to you." She began counting on her fingers. "You make more money than he does, you're more famous. In this life, *you* are the one with the bigger house and the fancier carriage. So let's just call it even, okay?"

"But it's not even," I argued, just for the sake of arguing, because when it came to Aaron, I couldn't seem to let anything go. "He has you."

Why was I saying this? I didn't want Katelyn for myself. Not truly. I loved her—yes, I always would—but a long time ago I realized that the thing I loved was our friendship and the family she had created…with my brother. The family she had allowed me to become a part of. When it came to Aaron and me, she was the bridge and the peacekeeper.

Besides, I loved my life, just as it was. I couldn't imagine Katelyn as my wife. Maybe I had been able to imagine it at one time, but not now.

She scoffed. "Come on, Jack. You don't want me, not like that. You have an amazing life, and we're the best of friends, as we were always meant to be. Whatever torch you once carried for me is long gone out and you know it. This is between you and Aaron, and Lord knows he has tried to start over. You're the one who refuses to put the past behind you. Behind all of us."

The doors to the ballroom opened, and all the reporters began to file in.

Katelyn and I walked beside each other in silence. Like a physical heat coming off her, I could feel her frustration with me.

We moved into the room and sat down in the second row, each of us withdrawing our notepads and pens. The FBI spokesperson entered with a group of local police officers and rescue officials. They informed us that still, no survivors had been found. The rescue operation had officially become a recovery effort.

As I comprehended the pain of all this loss and the suffering of the family members, my ancient quarrels with my brother suddenly felt petty and irrelevant. So much about why we disliked each other was rooted in the past, from other lifetimes, eons ago. Why should any of that matter today, when I had everything I ever wanted and we were no longer enemies? We were brothers this time.

Well… I had almost everything I ever wanted. I was still a single man.

I glanced around the room. All these families, grieving for each other, devastated by loss…

Every day is a gift.

I thought about what Katelyn had told me—that Aaron had been out on the water since the night of the crash, helping in the search for survivors.

She was right. He was a good man, at least in this life. I'd always known that. I simply preferred not to openly acknowledge it, because I preferred to hold onto my resentment over old squabbles. For some reason, it made me feel complete—as if the world was exactly as it was supposed to be. I was the good guy and he was the villain— which was ridiculous. He wasn't a villain. We just happened to have loved the same woman on more than one occasion.

And it had been Katelyn's decision to choose Aaron over me. We couldn't both win. I had no true understanding of the bond they shared. I didn't understand it because I'd never experienced anything like it myself. At least not yet.

Although Meg Andrews aroused something in me that reminded me of what I once felt for Katelyn—a sense of connection. Maybe it would lead to something, or maybe not. We'd only just met, and she might disappear from my life as quickly as she entered it. That happened sometimes. People you connected with went away, either in a plane crash or by choice.

So maybe Katelyn had never been the real prize. At least not for me. Maybe that's what I needed to understand and accept.

I leaned a little closer to her. "I'll call him tonight," I said, "just to see how he's doing."

"Do you promise?"

"I promise."

She laid her hand on my wrist and gave it a squeeze of gratitude, just as the rescue official called for a moment of silence to grieve for those who were gone.

For the first time since I had met Katelyn in New York more than ten years earlier, I did not feel forlorn sitting next to her. I did not feel like the unlucky one. Today, I felt only gratitude for having her in my life. As a friend.

The moment of silence ended, and the FBI spokesman moved to the microphone. He immediately began to outline the history of Jaeger-Woodrow Airways and its connection to Marquee-Goldman—a bankrupt airline I was very familiar with.

The room erupted into a wild frenzy of questions. As soon as the press briefing came to an end, every reporter—myself included—made a mad dash for the door, because this story was just the tip of the iceberg.

Twenty-eight

Meg

"**O**f course, now everyone thinks it's negligence on the part of the airline," I said to my brother Wayne on the phone when we talked later that afternoon. "Either from poor security or some mechanical failure they caused through lazy or corrupt management. The notion that it might have been a terrorist bomb is no longer at the top of everyone's mind. They're pointing fingers at Reginald Harrison. But the fact is, we still don't know. It could very well have been a bomb. He could have been doing everything right, following all the rules, but sometimes… We just won't know until we have all the evidence."

"What *do* you know?" Wayne asked.

I stood in the enormous hangar, staring at the broken sections of the 747 that had been recovered from the water and delivered so far. My colleagues were bagging and tagging everything and entering the information into the computer system. Meanwhile, the larger front half of the aircraft which included the flight deck was still in the field and trees next to Jack's parents' house.

"Not much," I replied, "except that the plane disappeared from radar after both transponders went dead at the exact same second, and the pilots didn't even have a chance to make an emergency call. That means it was either a massive structural failure and complete loss of power, or a midair collision—which we know it wasn't—or it was an explosion. But caused by what? Either way, we have a big job ahead of us, piecing this thing together."

"You're going to be there awhile, I take it?"

"Yes. Weeks."

One of my team members approached me with a cup of coffee. I mouthed the words *thank you* and peeled back the plastic rim to take a sip.

"How about you?" I asked Wayne. "How are you holding up?"

I couldn't imagine piloting for a major commercial airline after something like this. How difficult it must be for the crew members to trust that everything would be all right after takeoff.

"I'm just glad I'm not working for Jaeger-Woodrow Airways," he replied. "I don't think anyone in the aviation community knew about their history. Harrison certainly kept it well hidden."

"I just hope we can get to the bottom of this," I replied as a giant, noisy flatbed truck pulled into the hangar, carrying a massive piece of the starboard wing and a section of the rear cargo hold. Two black cars drove in behind it. I suspected they were the explosive experts from the FBI that called earlier to say they were on their way, along with a few members of the CIA and the FAA.

"I need to go," I said. "Some important people just arrived."

We hung up, and I set down my coffee to go and greet them.

~ ◎

It wasn't easy to get anything done under the hectic pace of all the meetings with different groups and officials, and the constant ringing of my phone, where questions came at me from left, right and center.

Inside the hangar, members of my own team constantly approached me for assistance. Meanwhile, the FBI had their own forensics experts working on site. Because they were the lead agency on this crash, I had to be careful not to step on their toes or get in their way, or we could end up in a turf war. I had to remember the boundaries and provide support and expertise when it was requested. It wasn't always easy to do that when all I wanted to do was take charge, kick everyone out of there, and do it all myself. When it came to crash investigations, I was a bit of a control freak.

Shortly after 6:00 p.m., my phone rang again. This time it was Jack. Having not spoken to him all day—and knowing that CNN and other news networks were looking into the connections between Jaeger-Woodrow and Marquee-Goldman Airlines—I was quick to answer it. Maybe he knew something we didn't.

"Hello?"

"Hey, it's Jack," he said. "Can you get away for a quick bite to eat?"

"Not really," I replied, glancing at the clock on the wall. "They're bringing food here in a little while. But don't you have a show to do?"

"Yes, but I'd like to talk to you before then." He

paused. "How about a coffee? We can sit down, just for a few minutes. I'm not fishing for information. I actually have something I want to share with you. Something that might help on your end."

I glanced around. The place was crawling with the FBI and CIA. I wasn't sure they'd appreciate a CNN reporter walking in the door.

"Where are you now?" I asked.

"In my car, just leaving downtown Portland. I'm ten minutes away."

I glanced around again. "How about I meet you in the airport hotel, in the lobby area. Look for the big fireplace."

"Sounds good," he replied. "I'll see you shortly."

I ended the call and grabbed my purse, then let one of my guys know that I was stepping out for a few minutes.

Twenty-nine

I walked into the crowded hotel lobby and spotted Jack, already there, seated on one of the sofas in front of the fireplace. He wore a black turtleneck with a brown leather jacket and jeans, and was sitting forward with his elbows on his knees, texting busily.

I watched him for a moment, feeling half in a daze, as if I had suddenly become weightless and was floating off the ground. I wasn't sure if the reason was my fascination with him as a celebrity—or simply as a very handsome man—or if it was pure mental exhaustion.

Putting one foot in front of the other, I approached him. "Hey."

He glanced up, slid his phone into his jacket pocket, and like a true, old-fashioned gentleman, he rose to his feet to greet me. He waited until I was seated before he sat down as well.

"Thanks for meeting me," he said. "I'll try not to keep you. I imagine you're pretty busy over there."

I shrugged. "It's all right. With the FBI taking the lead on this, it's not as big a deal for me to slip out for a few minutes. I'm glad you called."

He regarded me intently for a moment. "How are you doing today? Better?"

I inhaled deeply and rested my arm along the back of the sofa. "Yes. I really needed that sleep last night. It helped a lot."

"Good," he replied. "But it's still been rough today, hasn't it. They keep upping the death toll, and it's so hard on the families, having to identify their loved ones when there's…" He paused. "Not much to identify." Jack closed his eyes and pinched the bridge of his nose.

Something possessed me. I couldn't help myself. I leaned closer and laid my hand lightly on his knee. "Are *you* doing okay?"

He opened his eyes, and to my surprise, took hold of my hand and entwined his fingers through mine. My whole body buzzed with physical awareness. The sensation rushed all the way down to my toes and my heart began to race. It felt so good to touch him, to share the grief, to comfort each other in this small way.

"Life is unfair sometimes," he said. "It doesn't make any sense."

"I know."

"Have you ever lost someone close to you?" he asked.

I thought about it for a moment and realized how lucky I was to have been so fortunate in this lifetime.

"Just two of my grandparents," I replied, "but that was different. They were old and we expected it. We had time to prepare ourselves. But this… Something so sudden and unexpected and…*violent*. I've seen it up close, Jack, and you're right, it is unfair. Especially when you learn about the young children who died, and think about how awful it must have been for the parents in those final moments, not being able to do anything about it, or take away the fear." I looked away.

Heads bowed, neither of us spoke for a few seconds.

"I know that *you've* lost people close to you," I said. "In Afghanistan."

"Yes," he replied, "and I also lost a good friend when I was thirteen. Which is why I wanted to talk to you."

Curious, I inclined my head.

"First off," Jack said, "Thank you for the advance warning about the press conference this morning. That was a doozy. Reg Harrison…"

I nodded. "The FBI is all over it. They're looking into his business affairs, while my team is helping them investigate the airline's safety procedures. We're checking up on how well they've been adhering to FAA rules and regulations—among other things."

I realized Jack and I were still holding hands, and he was stroking my knuckle gently with his thumb. Maybe it was inappropriate—considering we were professionals working separately on an important investigation, and we barely knew each other—but I didn't care. I couldn't believe how good it felt. I didn't want him to stop. I just wanted to sit there all night long, and keep doing this.

"Will this news affect how you do your job?" he asked.

"Not really. I mean, of course I have to keep it in mind, but I'm a structures specialist, so I have to stay focused on what's in front of me—the wreckage in the hangar. But if other teams have specific information to relay, it might help me zero in on certain areas."

Jack continued to hold my hand in his. "Well, I don't know if this will be any help to you at all, but I just spent the past few hours reading an accident report from 1984."

My brow furrowed with a mixture of interest and concern. "Really? Which one?"

I was well aware that the NTSB accident reports were published on our website and made available to the public. We had been working steadily over the past number of years to publish older reports.

"It was a Marquee-Goldman crash that happened in Arizona," Jack explained. "I have a personal connection to it because my best friend and her whole family died in that crash. I was thirteen at the time."

"I'm so sorry. Was that the friend you just mentioned?"

He nodded and didn't say anything for a few seconds. Then his eyes met mine. "I never knew much about the particulars back then because I was just a kid and information wasn't as accessible as it is today. All I knew was that there was a fire that caused an explosion just before the plane landed. For a while, there was some thought that it might have been a bomb, but later, my mother told me it was an accident—that something in the cargo hold had caused the fire. I never knew what it was at the time. She never said."

"It was oxygen tanks," I told him.

I knew this because I had studied most of the major airline crashes over the duration of my career, even the ones that occurred before I was born.

"That's right," Jack replied. "According to the report, they were loaded into the cargo hold without proper precautions because the airline had a habit of blatantly disregarding safety procedures. The crash was blamed on human factors. Evidently, the delivery guys from PineTech—the oxygen supplier—and the baggage handlers weren't properly trained. They were cutting corners, trying to save time."

"Yes," I said, as the details of the report came back to me. "If memory serves me correctly, the person responsible was nineteen, and his only work experience had been a summer job mowing lawns. They paid him minimum wage and gave him half a day's training. He didn't secure the canisters like he should have."

"So you're familiar with that crash," Jack said, seeming suddenly energized.

"Yes, but I wouldn't have thought about it if you hadn't mentioned it. And it was almost a decade later that Marquee-Goldman went out of business because they were constantly lax in their safety procedures and they failed to implement our recommendations. They just didn't seem to care. It was criminal, if you ask me, that two more crashes had to occur before they were finally grounded and forced out of business."

"Yes, it *was* criminal," Jack agreed.

"So why are you telling me this?" I asked. "Do you think there's a connection between that accident and this one?"

"I don't think anything," he replied, making it clear that he wasn't throwing accusations around or speculating like the so-called "experts" on the Internet, who had their own theories about the crash, without ever seeing the evidence for themselves.

"And maybe," Jack continued, "if the FBI has begun digging into Reg Harrison's business affairs, they already know what I'm about to tell you, but I wanted to bring it up just in case. You can pass the information along to the right people if you think it's relevant."

I sat forward slightly. "What information?"

Jack reached into his jacket pocket and withdrew one of

his own business cards and a ball point pen. He wrote something down on the back of it and handed it to me.

"In 1984," he said, "the company that supplied the oxygen tanks that caused the fire was called PineTech. They went out of business after what happened to that flight in Arizona. But this afternoon, I had some of our people do some research, and it turns out that PineTech was a subsidiary of another of Harrison's umbrella corporations, and that same corporation—which still exists and is based in Switzerland—now operates another oxygen supply company called Oxy-GeoTech. Interestingly, they service a number of the major European airlines, and also sell oxygen supplies to hospitals."

I took the card and flipped it over to see what Jack had written on the back: *Oxy-GeoTech*.

"I think I see what you're getting at."

Jack slipped the pen back into his pocket. "I have no idea if this same company supplies oxygen to Jaeger-Woodrow Airways, or if oxygen had anything to do with this crash, or if it was another case of improper storage of something in the cargo hold that caused the plane to go down, but it might be worth looking into. If Harrison is still operating an airline without giving a hoot about safety, I'd hate to think history has repeated itself. If that's the case, he really needs to be stopped."

"I agree." I touched my finger to the card. "Thank you for this. I will definitely mention it to the FBI and the rest of my team, and get them to find out if there were any canisters on board that came from this company." I slipped the card into my purse. "I'm really sorry about your friend. I know it was a long time ago, but something like this must bring it all back."

"It does," Jack replied, rising to his feet as I stood. "Reading that accident report made me think about her and imagine what her last moments must have been like."

We regarded each other intently, and I felt a heated wave of desire course through me. It was not just a physical desire…although I did feel an incredible physical attraction to him. But it was more than that. It was a need to continue this conversation. I wanted to keep talking to Jack about his friend who had died, and so many other things—his childhood, his life experiences, his work. I wanted to know everything about him.

I wanted to sit close to him, lay my head on his shoulder, curl up against him and tell him about my conversation with Malcolm that morning and how it had frustrated me. I wanted to ask Jack what he thought I should do. I wanted to hear him tell me again that there was more to life than work.

Although clearly, I already knew it.

Nervously, I cleared my throat. "I should probably get back now."

"Of course." We began to walk out of the lobby together, but we were interrupted by a young couple who approached Jack. They told him they were "huge fans" and wanted to have their picture taken with him. Jack graciously agreed, and they posed while I snapped the picture on the woman's phone.

A moment later, Jack and I stood outside the hotel, under the overhang at the entrance. The roar of an airplane taking off on the runway nearby was thunderous in my ears, and I looked to the left to watch its ascent toward the sunset.

Jack waved to his driver, and I waved to mine. Both cars pulled up.

"What time will you be finished tonight?" Jack asked.

"I'm not sure," I replied. "Probably not until sometime after midnight. Then Gary will insist that we all go back to the hotel and get some sleep. How about you?"

"I have my show to do," he replied. "Then I'll probably head to my parents' place." His driver approached, but Jack turned to look at me before he got into his car. "The offer still stands if you want to have a drink later, or any time. Or if you just want to call and chat for a bit. It doesn't matter how late it is. And I'm not trying to get the inside scoop from you. I promise."

"I wouldn't think that," I said, as my driver pulled up behind Jack's car.

Jack walked me to it and opened the door for me. He was such a gentleman. I felt a little breathless as he stood there, so handsome in the glow of the summer twilight, his gaze roaming all over my face.

"Can I ask you a really weird and totally inappropriate question?" he said.

I was momentarily taken aback, and very curious about what he wanted to ask. "Go ahead."

"How old are you?"

My head drew back in surprise, because it *was* a strange question, not at all what I had expected. "I'm thirty-one. Why?"

He shook his head, as if embarrassed, and looked down at his shoes. I found myself staring at the top of his head— the thick, wavy dark hair blowing in the breeze.

"No reason," he replied. "I don't know. I was just curious. That was stupid."

"It wasn't stupid," I replied, "because I'd love to ask how old *you* are, except I already know. You're forty-five."

His eyes lifted, and they were intense and penetrating. "How do you know that?"

"Because I googled you," I explained with a sheepish grin. "Don't be freaked out. I'm not stalking you or anything. I was just curious, too. I don't know why. You're an interesting person."

Electricity sparked in the air between us, and this time, there was no doubt in my mind. I knew it wasn't just me. He was feeling something, too. That awareness caused a commotion in me...an intoxicating thrill.

Although it was long past time for me to get into the car, I hesitated because I didn't want to say good-bye to Jack. I just wanted to keep standing there, to remain in his presence a little longer.

It was a fierce, inescapable desire, and it made me think of Malcolm again—but not because I felt guilty. To the contrary, this was making me realize how little Malcolm truly meant to me.

And how little I meant to him.

It was the same for both of us. Our relationship had become a habit. A safe, easy habit, with no passion or longing or thoughts about the future. When we were apart, it was simply "out of sight, out of mind."

"I wish we were meeting under different circumstances," Jack said quietly, as if to hide our conversation from my driver.

"Me, too." All thoughts of Malcolm vanished from my brain as I continued to stand there. All I could think about was what it would feel like to kiss Jack. I couldn't take my eyes off his lips. I just wanted to step into his arms.

"I should go," I said, feeling a critical need to bolt

before something actually happened between us, because I didn't want to be a cheater.

I got into the car. "Good luck with your show tonight," I said. "Maybe we'll talk later."

Jack closed the door and stepped back.

As my driver pulled away, I laid a hand on my belly, where a gazillion butterfly wings were flapping wildly, causing a rush of heated exhilaration in my veins. I couldn't seem to stop my heart from racing, and it aroused an unexpected euphoria in me.

How was a feeling of euphoria even possible under circumstances like these? When I was in the middle of a crash investigation?

My emotions were spinning out of control. It wasn't something I was accustomed to because, out of necessity, I had honed my ability to detach.

This scared me.

A lot.

CHAPTER

Thirty

Jack

As I stood on the curb outside the airport hotel, watching Meg head back to the aircraft hangar, I told myself to get a grip.

Don't be crazy, Jack. Just because you're hot for the smart female crash investigator doesn't mean it's anything more. You're attracted to her because she's beautiful and there's some chemistry there. This sort of thing happens all the time, especially under intense circumstances like these.

It doesn't mean she's Millicent.

I started walking to my car and got in, lounged back on the leather seat and tapped my finger on my knee.

"Let's head back to the hotel," I said to Curtis, knowing I'd have to contact my producer soon about the show. But I needed a minute first. A personal minute.

I raked both my hands through my hair, feeling frustrated as I looked out the window at another plane taking off into the sky, its engines deafening in the peace of the early evening. The sunset was incredible and the clouds were lit up with splashes of pink and red. It was a beautiful sight to behold, yet I felt like I was losing my mind.

Why was I so wound up?

Probably because there was no way to know if it was true—if Meg Andrews was actually the reincarnation of my friend, Millicent. What proof did I have to even suppose it?

I took a breath and went over the facts.

Meg was thirty-one, which meant she was born the year after Millicent died.

But that wasn't proof of anything. Lots of people were born that year.

Meg had a fear of flying that she couldn't explain, and she experienced extreme symptoms of anxiety at a crash site.

But who wouldn't? That didn't mean she died in a plane crash in a previous life. It just meant she was sensitive to tragedy. Most good people were.

But why choose this line of work? I wondered, still tapping my finger on my knee.

I had asked her that once, and she told me she had fought through her fear to get her pilot's license and had become hooked on aviation. She later said she "lived and breathed" airline investigations. That she was obsessed.

Why the obsession? Interestingly, that was her word, not mine.

I thought back to the moment when it first occurred to me that she might be Millicent. It had struck me only a few hours earlier, while I was reading the accident report and began to recall my friendship with Millicent in the seventh grade.

It wasn't anything specific that caused me to make the connection, just a feeling that if Millicent were alive today, she would be just like Meg, because Millicent had also possessed a personal drive that bordered on obsession when it came to anything she wanted to have or do.

School, for instance. Millicent was a high achiever in that area.

The clubhouse. She was unstoppable in our quest to build it.

And Aaron. She had nearly lost her sanity trying to make my brother fall in love with her.

Millicent had a way of attacking things, and Meg struck me as the same. Their personalities were freakishly similar. And whenever I looked into her eyes, I felt like we already knew each other very well. It had been that way from the first moment.

But still—and I told myself over and over—it didn't mean Meg was Millicent. They could be similar without being the same. And maybe it was just the frustration of lust because she was completely unattainable. She was already in a relationship—a nine-year relationship with a surgeon.

I shook my head at myself. Why couldn't I learn this lesson: that it was pointless to live in the past, always trying to recapture something that was never meant to be? Like with Katelyn.

What mattered was the here and now, and what lay ahead in *this* life.

So even if I was overwhelmingly attracted to Meg, for whatever reason, I shouldn't be imagining that she was someone else. She was just Meg—thirty-one-year-old Meg—an unavailable crash investigator I found heart-stoppingly attractive.

Damn. Talk about life being unfair.

CHAPTER

Thirty-one

Meg

As soon as I arrived back at the hangar, I called Gary and told him everything Jack had gleaned from the report about the Arizona crash in 1984 and the oxygen supply company that had caused the accident. I asked Gary to share the information with the FBI and also have our team look into what had been loaded into the cargo hold of Flight 555—which my highly skilled team was surely doing already—but to specifically be on the lookout for any connections to Reg Harrison's company, Oxy-GeoTech.

Hanging up the phone, I returned to the reconstruction area, where we were still cataloguing pieces from the wing and parts of the fuselage. I could feel my body temperature rising with frustration. I felt restless and short-tempered.

I wanted to start putting this aircraft back together now, to see exactly what kind of explosion we were dealing with, but everything was spread out all over the floor, and we still didn't have the tail or any major portions of the rear fuselage, not to mention the flight data recorder. I couldn't help but feel annoyed by all the holdups. I was consumed by impatience, because there was something about this crash that was eating away at me, more so than other crashes I'd worked on. I wanted to be at the finish line, at the point where we had concrete answers and were ready to publish a report. But I knew I couldn't rush it. I had to be thorough.

As I stood looking around at the unsolved puzzle—at all the tiny, battered, and torn-up pieces of metal spread out on the floor—I felt weariness at a bone-deep level.

I wanted this finished so that I could move on.

But move on to what, exactly? Another crash?

The thought of that caused my mood to take a dark turn, even though it was already in a gloomy, agitated place.

Would there ever come a day when there would be no more plane crashes? No more frightening, untimely deaths and paralyzing grief for those left behind?

Every day, that's all I wanted. That's what drove me— the inescapable need to prevent the next disaster from happening.

But was it even possible in this world we lived in? Or would I live out the rest of my days with this frustration, always feeling a sense of failure whenever another plane went down and I had to pack up and travel to another morbid crash site and start all over again?

Knowing that assurances of total safety would never be possible in the world of aviation, I dove into my work that night as I always did, with ferocious concentration and focus, wanting to tackle this investigation and find the answers the families so desperately needed.

After about three hours of inspection and cataloguing— and answering dozens of questions about the tiniest details from different workers—my cell phone rang.

When I checked the call display, my stomach turned over with dread.

~*O*

"*Hey...*" I said in that quiet, intimate voice Malcolm would expect when I answered his call. "How are you doing?"

I walked through the giant open door of the hangar to stand outside on the tarmac, where I could watch planes in the distance, taxiing to and from the runway. A nearby truck sounded its back-up alarm as its reverse lights came on.

It was completely dark now and the sky was clear with a half moon.

"I'm doing okay," Malcolm replied. "I just got home a little while ago and I'm about to dig into a giant container of Pad Thai."

"That sounds yummy." I looked down at the worn hem of my trousers and my black leather shoes as I paced in small circles in front of the hangar.

Suddenly, I found myself trying to remember the last time I wore a skirt or a sundress. Or flip flops? God, it was the middle of summer. When had I last painted my toenails?

More importantly, why didn't I have a normal life, like most people?

"How was work today?" I asked Malcolm.

"Oh, you know. Same old, same old. Did a couple of knee replacements and put a pin in a guy's elbow. How about you?"

I breathed deeply and looked up at the sky, then turned my gaze toward a tiny, distant light—a plane on its final approach, still many miles away.

"Do you ever think about what it would be like to die in

a plane crash?" I asked Malcolm. "Do you wonder what you would be thinking when the plane was going down, in those last few seconds?"

"Jeez… What kind of question is that?"

I cupped my forehead in my hand and shook my head. "I don't know. I'm sorry. It's been a stressful day. I must be losing it."

Malcolm was quiet for a moment, then surprisingly he answered the question. "I'd probably freak out about who was going to cover my shift the next day. I'd be fumbling with my phone, trying to make a quick call to let them know I wouldn't be in."

I stopped in my tracks and felt a sudden rush of anger—first of all, that he would actually think *that* in his final moments. Second of all, that he was making fun of this. "Seriously?"

He scoffed. "No, Meg, I'm joking."

But I wasn't sure I believed him. He probably *would* think about his job, and not about me.

Another plane took off noisily.

"You must be at the airport?" Malcolm said.

"Yeah, we've set up shop in the hangar." I began to pace again, and looked down at the toes of my shoes as I put one foot in front of the other.

Left, right, left, right…

It's time for us to break up.

How odd that I felt no regret or sadness over the fact that I had finally come to the conclusion that this relationship wasn't worth fighting for. It hadn't been working for many years, and maybe Malcolm knew it too. Maybe that's why I wasn't worried about hurting him.

Or maybe I was numb inside. Clinically detached,

emotionally. Incapable of feeling my own personal pain because I was constantly surrounded by the pain of others and I'd had to protect myself.

"Do you miss me?" I asked Malcolm, just to see what he would say.

He laughed awkwardly. "Of course. Why would you ask that?"

I shrugged. "I don't know. You never tell me that you miss me."

"You never tell me either," he replied.

I couldn't be upset with him over that response, because it was completely true.

And I *wasn't* upset. Not in the least. That was the problem. I felt only indifferent about Malcolm's lack of desire to hold me in his arms, to kiss me, or tell me that he loved me.

At the same time, I had to question *why* I was having these thoughts today, when there were so many other things on my mind, crash-related.

But of course, I knew the answer. This was Jack's fault. Just because I knew how to detach emotionally when it counted, didn't mean I couldn't recognize what was causing this disruption in me. I felt passion and excitement for the first time in years—I felt *alive*—and suddenly it seemed like such a waste, not to feel this kind of passion with the boyfriend I was spending my life with.

Life was short and oh, so fragile. I was squandering it. So was he.

And really…*boyfriend*? What a childish word to describe our relationship when we were both in our early thirties and had been together for nine years.

"Can I ask you something else?" I said, tilting my head back to look up at the stars again.

"Sure." I heard the microwave door open and close as Malcolm withdrew his Pad Thai. I imagined him carrying it to the kitchen table with oven mitts, getting ready to tell me that he'd talk to me tomorrow, so that he could eat his supper while it was still hot.

"Why don't we ever talk about marriage?" I asked. "Is it not something you want?"

Malcolm was silent for a few seconds. "Is it something *you* want? I didn't think so. You've always said you were married to your job."

I let out a heavy sigh, because I had indeed said that, once. And it wasn't as if my womb was suddenly aching for a baby tomorrow, or that I wanted to move to the suburbs and get a house with a white picket fence, and become a happy housewife and soccer mom.

But if I ever wanted children—eventually—I couldn't continue to coast along this current path of status quo. There was a biological clock to consider. I was nothing, if not scientific and practical.

"I did say that," I replied, "but I was younger then." I wandered around to the side of the hangar where there was a patch of grass overcome by dandelions that had gone to seed.

"What are you saying, Meg? That you want to get married?"

"Do *you*?" I asked, knowing it was a very dangerous question, because what if he said yes? I already knew that a wedding with Malcolm was not what I wanted.

He didn't, of course, say yes—which was why I'd felt safe asking. I knew.

"I can't imagine how we'd make *that* work," he replied with a hint of humor, obviously trying to steer this conversation away from where it was heading. "You're always on the road, Meg, and I'm always in the OR. One of us would have to give up something, and we both love our jobs."

Love?

No, I didn't love my job. It made me throw up. But for some reason, I was compelled to keep doing it. Every day, I had to force myself to be strong, to find a way to get through it.

I almost said "Maybe I *want* to give this up" but I held my tongue, because I didn't want Malcolm to think I was pushing for him to propose to me, because that wasn't what I wanted from this conversation.

"You're right," I calmly said. "It's true. We care more about our jobs than we do about each other."

"Well, I wouldn't put it *that* way," he replied.

I closed my eyes and breathed the cool night air. "I would. But it's okay, Malcolm. I'm not mad about it."

He was silent. In shock, probably.

"What are you trying to say?" he finally asked.

I began to stroll back around to the front of the hangar, where people were coming and going and phones were ringing, even at this late hour. "That I think it's time we take a long hard look at our relationship and decide if it's worth continuing."

I heard the sound of his fork clinking against the plate. "I don't understand. What's going on? Everything was fine the last time you were here."

"Yes, it was," I agreed. "But I want more than *fine*, Malcolm. I want to feel joy and excitement. I want to have a life outside of my work…maybe take vacations and travel. I want to feel grateful to be alive. Shouldn't we all feel grateful? Shouldn't we be in awe?"

"In awe of *what*?" he asked with a note of impatience.

"Of *life*!" I shouted. "Of this beautiful world! *God*, I'm surrounded by tragedy all the time. I want to be able to celebrate the good stuff, because I know it's out there. I need to see it. Experience it."

I heard nothing but the sound of his fork clinking against his plate.

"I'm surprised to hear you saying all this right now," Malcolm finally said in a quiet voice that sounded almost disappointed. "You're always so…*intense* when you start a new investigation. You don't want to talk to me. That's why I give you space. I just wait until you come around and want to visit again."

I thought about that, and couldn't argue with him. It was how we always were. We backed off when the other was immersed in work. And it wasn't just me. It was a two-way street because I backed off plenty of times for him, too.

In that way, we'd seemed like the perfect match, but maybe it wasn't healthy for me to be with someone exactly like me. Maybe I should be with someone who wouldn't allow me to disappear into my work. Someone who would remind me that there is more to life than plane crashes and tragedy.

"Maybe space isn't what I need," I said. "Maybe I need to feel some…*connection*."

"You don't feel that with me?" he asked, matter-of-factly, as if he were gathering information on a chart.

"Not really," I gently replied. "I usually feel like you're too busy or pre-occupied, so I don't push to get close."

"You can always talk to me," he said flatly.

"I'm talking to you now."

I don't know what I expected from him in that moment,

or what I wanted him to say. Was it even possible to build a soulful connection to Malcolm when I'd never felt it before? Would he suddenly step up and...*do what?* Hop on a plane and fly here immediately to hold me in his arms and say that he wanted more out of life, too?

No. Malcolm would never do that. He was content with things the way they were, and he had never been a terribly introspective person. He was a man of science. Soulful connections had no meaning for him.

Neither of us spoke for an excruciating moment. I looked in at the steady activity in the hangar where everyone was working hard to gather all the evidence from this disaster and try to make sense of it.

"Well, I'm not sure what to say to you," Malcolm replied at last. "It kind of feels like you're telling me that you're not happy with what we have."

I spoke gently. "It's been good all these years. I just feel like I need something more."

"Like what? Do you want to go on a cruise or something? Is that what you're saying?"

He truly had no idea what I was talking about, and I was quite certain there was no way to make him understand.

"I don't know," I replied, giving up the effort.

"I don't want to lose you, Meg."

"Why not?" I asked. "Do you believe you couldn't live without me? Because I don't think that's the case. I think you'd get over me pretty quickly and maybe meet someone else who makes you feel—I don't know—more than what you feel with me. Maybe we both need to broaden our horizons."

There was another pause. "Why now?"

I considered that for a moment. "I don't know. Maybe

it's something about this crash. It's hitting me harder than others. It's making me think about life. I think we all need to make the most of it while we're here."

Again, we were silent for a long time, neither of us wanting to hang up, because that would feel very final.

It was a fellow NTSB worker who helped me over that hurdle. She was a young summer student, like I had been once. She walked toward me uncertainly.

"Can I ask you a question?" she whispered with a grimace, not wanting to interrupt my call.

I nodded at her and said to Malcolm, "I'm sorry but I have to go. Let's talk again tomorrow, okay?"

He agreed, and I ended the call, dealt with the question and returned to work.

By the time I arrived back at the hotel, it was past midnight and I was exhausted, both physically and mentally. All I wanted to do was curl up in a ball and go straight to bed, but as soon as I changed into my pajamas—which consisted of a tank top and loose bottoms—a text came in.

At first I thought it was Malcolm, wanting to fix what was broken between us. But it wasn't Malcolm. It was Jack.

I sat down on the edge of the bed and read: *Hey, are you done for the day? Feel like talking?*

My thumbs worked swiftly across the screen as I typed my reply: *I just got in a few minutes ago, and yes I do feel like talking. Call me?*

Seven seconds later, my phone rang.

"It's good to hear your voice right now," I softly said, which was an incredibly intimate greeting, and hardly appropriate, considering he was a professional acquaintance and I was still in a relationship with Malcolm.

Sort of.

"It's good to hear yours, too," Jack replied, his voice husky and low. "I thought about you a lot today."

My heart began to pound like a piston because I didn't know where this was heading. All I knew was that I felt something intense for Jack Peterson, and I didn't want to simply let it pass me by. I was tired of being disengaged.

"Did you make any progress at the hangar today?" he asked.

"A bit," I replied. "We should be able to start the reconstruction fairly soon. And I told Gary about the Arizona crash and the connection to Reg Harrison's oxygen company in Switzerland. The FBI is looking into all his business affairs, and my team at the airport has been going over everything that was loaded into the cargo hold with a fine tooth comb. So far, though, there's no record of any shipments from Oxy-GeoTech."

"That's good, I guess. Although it doesn't get you any closer to the answers." He paused. "You sound tired, Meg. Are you doing okay?"

Sliding my body up the length of the mattress to rest my head on the pillows, I crossed my legs at the ankles and fiddled with the red draw-string on my floral pajama bottoms. "I'm all right, considering I pretty much broke up with Malcolm tonight."

There was a long pause on the other end of the line while I waited for Jack to respond.

"Really," he said at last. "What happened?"

As I twirled the string around my finger, I found myself wanting to confess my innermost feelings to him.

"Nothing, really, which has been the problem for a while now—the fact that we both feel completely indifferent about our relationship. It's not like we had a big fight or anything, and I don't even know what sparked the conversation."

I sat up straighter on the bed and continued. "Maybe it's because of what you and I talked about the other day— about taking vacations. It made me re-evaluate a few things. Or maybe it's all the crashes I've been working on over the past decade, finally pushing me over the edge, making me realize how fragile life is. Either way, when I tried to talk to Malcolm about it, he just didn't get it. He doesn't think anything's wrong with what we have. He's happy with his life, just the way it is, and how I fit into it—which is in a very limited way."

"I'm sorry to hear that," Jack said. "So are you officially broken up?"

I pursed my lips, thinking about it. In my heart, it was over for me—I suppose it had been over for a long time—

but I hadn't been completely clear about that with Malcolm. I just hadn't been able to bring myself to blindside him with a sudden break-up he never saw coming.

"Not yet," I replied. "I suggested we talk about it again tomorrow, but I don't think anything will change. At least not on my end."

"You never know," Jack replied. "He might realize what he's about to lose, then panic, and decide to do whatever it takes to hold on to you. God knows, that's what I would do."

I felt a warm glow blossom inside of me. "That's sweet, Jack. But he's not like you. Honestly, I don't think it will make much difference to him if I'm not a part of his life anymore. I can't imagine him being heartbroken over it. He's the least romantic person I know. He's not the type to fly here with a bouquet of flowers and try to change my mind. He's too consumed by his work."

"Maybe he'll surprise you."

I slumped down on the pillows. "Maybe."

But I didn't believe he would.

Jack was quiet for a moment. "Maybe this is selfish of me, but I hope he *doesn't* surprise you."

The very air around me felt electrified as I pondered his words. My insides jangled with excitement.

"I know it's late," Jack added, "but do you want to get a drink and talk some more? I could meet you in the hotel bar."

I rolled onto my side and cradled the phone against my cheek. "Part of me wants to say yes, because I'd really love to see you right now and pour out my heart and soul. But I'm still with Malcolm, officially. I don't want to do anything that might make me feel like I'm being unfaithful—even though it's over between us, and I'm sure he knows it. Besides, I'm about to nod off. It was a stressful day."

Jack replied in a quiet, genuine voice. "I understand. So I guess that means it's too soon for me to ask you out on a proper date?"

I chuckled softly. "A little too soon, yes. But please keep it in mind."

"When might be a good time?" he asked. "How long are we talking about here? Days? Weeks? I'd just like to have a ballpark figure so I can plan accordingly."

I laughed again, very softly into the phone. "I'm not sure. I still need to talk this through with Malcolm, and make sure he understands that there's no future."

"Okay," Jack calmly replied. "And no pressure, but Meg…I want you to know that…I don't know what's going on here between us, but I can't get you out of my head. It's making me crazy. I'll go nuts if I can't see you again, very soon."

There was something seductive in the deep timbre of his voice, and it sent my pulse into overdrive. Liquid heat flooded my body and I felt restless. I wanted to get up off the bed and dance around the hotel room.

I closed my eyes, bit my lower lip, and spoke breathlessly. "I feel the same way. Whenever I see you, I feel completely…"

He waited for me to finish, but I was too shy to be honest with him. Too reserved to tell him that all I wanted to do was tackle him and rip off all his clothes, hold him down and kiss him hard.

When was the last time I'd felt anything as wild as that?

But of course, how could I forget? Back in college, I'd fallen for a bad boy and went through a phase that hadn't ended well, but at least it taught me a few lessons. That's how I ended up with Malcolm, who was the exact opposite of Kyle—mature, responsible, but without any zest for life.

Surely, there had to be a happy medium in there somewhere.

"I think I might have a bit of a crush on you," I told Jack, knowing I had to finish what I'd begun.

"I'm glad," he replied in that low, quiet voice that gave me goose bumps, "because I have a crush on you, too."

A siren wailed somewhere in the city, reminding me where I was and why I was there. Despite all my preaching to Malcolm a few short hours ago—about wanting to take time to enjoy life—I couldn't simply forget about my job either. I needed to know what caused this crash. Tomorrow, I would be in the meeting room at 7:00 a.m. to take part in a morning briefing with Gary and the rest of the team. I couldn't be distracted.

Rolling onto my back, I covered my eyes with my hand and inhaled deeply.

"I can feel a 'but' coming on," Jack said, and I began to believe that he actually *could* read my mind.

"It's a timing thing," I said with a heavy note of regret. "And it's not just because of Malcolm. It's the investigation. I don't want to drop the ball right now. I need to stay focused. See it through. You get that, right?"

Was I insane? Jack Peterson just told me that he had a crush on me, and I was basically telling him to back off. *Had I learned nothing?*

"Let's just take it slow," I added, mentally kicking myself in the pants. "Give me a few days, okay?"

"Days," Jack replied, sounding relieved. "Sure. I can wait a few days. But I have to fly back to New York at the end of the week. When will you be going back to Washington?"

"I don't know," I replied. "I could be here for weeks if we don't find answers right away. But I don't want to wait that long to see you again."

There. I wasn't a total lost cause. At least I had the sense not to let myself screw this up completely.

Nor did I want to keep living like I had been living. I wanted more out of life, and in particular, I wanted to be with Jack and see if this connection I felt was as meaningful as it seemed.

Because it *did* feel meaningful, which said a lot, coming from me. I was a crash investigator and concrete evidence was everything. We never made assumptions or formed conclusions based on a hunch or a "feeling."

Yet tonight, I felt as if all the moments of my life had brought me to this place, to meet Jack Peterson under these exact circumstances—and I had no explanation for it. There was nothing the least bit concrete about what I was feeling.

"Let's have dinner before you leave," I said. "I'll find a way to take a few hours off."

"My flight leaves Sunday morning," he told me. "How about Saturday night?"

"Yes."

It was 1:00 in the morning, and I couldn't stifle a yawn.

"Meg," Jack said, "you should get some sleep. I'll call you on Saturday and we'll talk more then." He paused. "There's actually…something else I want to discuss with you."

"What is it?" I asked, sitting up on the bed because I could tell by the tone of his voice that it was important. More information about the crash, perhaps?

"I don't want to get into it now," he said. "You're tired."

I couldn't help probing. "You're not secretly married, are you?"

"No, it's nothing like that," he said with a laugh. "I'm very single, and have been for a while. I probably shouldn't have said anything. Now you'll be curious."

"I am, a little. Does it have something to do with the crash?"

There was a long pause.

"Sort of. But not Flight 555. The other one. The Arizona crash. The one where my friend died. But listen, it can wait. It has nothing to do with your investigation. It's more of a personal matter."

"Okay," I finally said. "In that case, I'll wait until Saturday."

"Good. I'll see you then."

We hung up, and I shut off the light to go to sleep. I couldn't drift off, however, because I was completely wired, unable to keep from imagining what it might be that Jack wanted to discuss with me.

Maybe he was seeking a clearer understanding about what happened to his friend. I understood that. I'd seen it a lot—the need for answers, the belief that some piece of information would somehow lessen the grief and provide closure.

But when it came to airline disasters, closure for the loved ones was often a pipe dream. It wasn't something you could just "get over" when someone explained the mechanics of why the plane had gone down. Most family members were left behind to continue asking *why* for the rest of their lives. But only God had the answer to that question.

After tossing and turning for almost an hour, and still thinking about what Jack wanted to talk about, I finally rose from bed and opened up my laptop. I logged into the NTSB website and searched for the accident report from the Arizona crash in 1984.

It was a 250-page document, and because it was so late and I needed my sleep, I debated about whether or not I should start reading it. My eyes were burning, yet my brain was firing on all cylinders.

In the end, I decided to take a closer look at the report, and see if anything jumped out at me.

CHAPTER

Thirty-three

Jack

"**A**re you crazy?" Katelyn said to me the following morning when we bumped into each other at another press briefing in the hotel. "You only just met her and you don't have any proof. She'll think you're insane. Besides, you shouldn't jump to conclusions like that. Just because you're attracted to her doesn't mean you knew her in a previous life."

"In this life, actually," I clarified, as I sipped my coffee. "But you're probably right. She *will* think I'm insane."

Just then, the local police and medical examiner, along with a few members of the FBI, entered the room to deliver the latest information about the crash. Meg wasn't there. I knew she wouldn't be. She was at the airport hangar that morning, supervising the arrival of the cockpit and front half of the plane, which had just been removed from the field near my parents' house.

As far as the press briefing was concerned, there was some new information to convey, including the latest death toll and the continued search for human remains, wreckage, and the black box in the water.

We were told that hundreds of pathologists, dentists, and other medical technicians were arriving by the hour to assist in the identification process of the passengers' remains. You could have heard a pin drop in the room in that moment.

The FBI also revealed that they had not yet found any evidence of an explosive device on board the plane, and still, no terrorist groups had come forward to take credit for the disaster. The authorities assured everyone that they were still investigating all possible causes, but at this point, they were not ruling out some sort of mechanical failure.

There was no mention of improperly stored oxygen tanks, so I wondered if it had been a long shot on my part— making connections when there were none to be had— because of a personal bias. It could very well be the case, but I hoped that Meg would let me know if the information I'd shared with her turned out to be useful in some way.

When asked about the black boxes, the FBI explained that they were still searching the ocean floor, and hoped to have more information for us soon.

With that, the press briefing came to an end.

I walked out with Katelyn, and while we filtered through the door with the other reporters, she said, "When will we get to meet her?"

"Who, Meg?" I asked.

"Yes, Meg. Who else?"

I considered it for a moment. "I don't know. It depends on how things go on Saturday. Maybe I *am* just imagining things. Maybe she's just a normal woman. Someone I've never known before."

"If you ask me," Katelyn said, "that's how you should approach this, because you've always tried to maneuver your life based on memories from the past, trying to fit a square peg into a round hole, when what you really need to do is live this life for the first time, and stop imagining that the past has any significance when it comes to your future. Think about it, Jack. Most people have no knowledge of their past lives, and they get along just fine. They're happy. So forget about all of that and get to know this woman like normal people do on a first date."

I gave her a look. "We both know I'm not normal."

She smiled. "You're right about that. But normal is boring. We like you just the way you are."

We walked out of the hotel together and went back to work.

Thirty-four

Meg

I should have known better than to stay up half the night reading that accident report, because I was a complete mess that morning. And it was an important day. Not only was the front half of the aircraft being delivered to the hangar, but we were starting to make sense of the wreckage we had so far. I was chomping at the bit to start putting pieces together and see what sort of damage the explosion had caused, and get a better sense of where it had originated.

But I could barely think straight, and it was my own fault.

After I turned off the lights in my hotel room at 3:00 a.m. and finally fell asleep, I woke up from a terrible nightmare ninety minutes later.

In the dream, I was a passenger on the Arizona flight as it was going down, and I was watching the fire burn through the floor and fill the cabin with smoke. People were screaming, and a flight attendant pounded on the cockpit door, shouting at the pilots: "*We're on fire!*"

All of this, I had read in the accident report that was published online. The sound of the flight attendant's voice had been captured by the cockpit voice recorder, along with the pilots' distress calls to report the situation and request permission to make an emergency landing.

In the dream, however, I was a passenger, and I never knew such terror. The oxygen masks dropped from the overhead compartments and my mother fastened mine to my face.

"We'll be okay!" she said to me. I stared at her with wide eyes, trusting her, believing her totally and completely.

But then the plane took a sudden nose dive and rolled to the side.

In the dream, I don't remember the explosion. I only remember floating out of my body, flying upwards through the hull of the burning aircraft. I flew beside my mother, who left the aircraft at the same time, holding my hand, along with all the other passengers. It was quite a crowd floating out of there, all at the same time, together.

I saw blue sky and white clouds, and felt a wonderful sense of peace and community. I was so happy and relieved to be out of there. *Thank you, God…*

When I woke in my hotel room, however, I felt no peace, for I couldn't forget the fear and blinding panic as the plane went into a death spiral and everyone began screaming. I woke in a cold sweat, fighting to suck air into my lungs.

It was a familiar fear. I'd felt it every time I stepped onto a plane in my youth and sat down to buckle in.

That was before I forced myself to take hold of my fear and wrestle it into submission. When I learned how to fly on my own, it was the feeling of holding the yoke—managing the speed and the lift—that had cured me, because when I could do that I finally felt as if I were in control.

Now, here I stood in a hangar in Portland, Maine, many years later, staring at thousands of pieces of metal and an enormous front section of a 747, including the cockpit, while everyone was looking to me for answers. I wanted them more desperately than ever before.

Had there been a fire in the cargo hold? Was that what cut off all the power and caused the pilots to lose control? If so, what had caused the fire?

And where was that darn black box?

CHAPTER

Thirty-five

Jack

When I answered my phone, it was Katelyn.

"Drop everything," she said. "I just got a call from Aaron's foreman, Vince. They were out on the water helping with the recovery. He told me they just found the black box, but that Aaron's hurt."

"What do you mean, he's hurt?"

"I'm not sure," she replied with panic in her voice. "They're bringing him in now by helicopter. All I know is what Vince told me—that a speedboat with a photographer on board rammed into their boat. He was probably looking for the money-shot of the black box and wasn't looking where he was going. Vince said Aaron was distracted by something—he wouldn't tell me what—and that he hit his head and flew over the side, and they had to fish him out of the water. Vince said he was unconscious." She sounded frantic. "They're on the way to the hospital now. Oh, God, Jack... What if it's bad?"

"Where are you now?" I asked.

"I'm at the TV station, just heading out."

"I'm heading out, too. I'll be at the hospital in ten minutes," I told her.

"Keep your phone on."

"I will. See you in a bit."

I slid my phone into my pocket and hurried out the door.

~⊘

They were just wheeling the gurney into the ER when I ran into the hospital. I stopped in my tracks, unnerved by the sight of my unconscious brother lying flat with a brace fastened around his neck. His head was bandaged. There was a lot of blood.

"I'm his brother," I said, following alongside as they rushed Aaron toward a trauma room. They ignored me as they pushed through the doors. A nurse took hold of my arm.

"You'll have to wait out here," she said. "They're going to do everything they can."

I watched through a glass window, staring in disbelief as a team of doctors lifted Aaron off the gurney and onto an examination table. They immediately began hooking him up to monitors, while one doctor leaned over him and spoke firmly. "Can you hear me Mr. Peterson? Do you know where you are?"

Aaron gave no response. The doctor shook his head at one of the others. "Nothing."

I felt a sick knot twist in my gut as the nurse led me away to the waiting area.

Just then, Katelyn ran through the doors. Our eyes met. "Is he here?" she asked.

"Yes. They just took him into a trauma room."

"Is he awake?"

"No."

Her brow furrowed with concern. "Is he going to be okay?"

I stared at her for a few nerve-wracking seconds. "I don't know."

She covered her face with her hands, and walked straight into my arms.

Thirty-six

Meg

T he front section of the aircraft was just rolling into the hangar on the back of a giant flatbed truck when Gary called to me from the office. He was talking to someone on the phone, covering the mouthpiece with one hand.

"They found it!"

I turned away from the truck and started walking toward him. "You mean the black box?"

Still taking more information from the caller, he could only nod his head. He waved me over and I quickened my pace.

As soon as I entered the office, he closed the door behind me. I sat down on a chair. "Did they find the tail as well?" I asked in a whisper, trying not to interrupt. "And the rest of the plane?"

Gary held up a finger, signaling me to be quiet and patient until he finished. Then he said to the person on the other end of the line, "Okay, I got it. Yep, we'll be there soon."

He hung up and turned to me. "Good news. Both data recorders are on their way to Washington for analysis. And yes, they found what they believe is the rest of the aircraft, including the tail and what's left of the rear section of the fuselage, which they say is in small pieces, spread out over a very large area on the ocean floor."

"Shoot," I replied. "What about the port wing? Did they find that as well?"

He frowned. "No one could identify that because, as I said, everything is in pieces. I've asked if we can get cameras down there before we start bringing stuff up."

"Yes," I agreed. "I need to see exactly how she landed on the ocean floor. Can you get me out there so I can view the camera feed and supervise the recovery?"

Gary nodded. "I've already ordered a chopper to take us out. Can you be ready to go in ten minutes?"

"Of course." I stood up and went to find Brent, to let him know he'd be in charge at the hangar until I returned.

A short time later, Gary and I were climbing into the helicopter, which would take us out over the choppy Atlantic to where the Coast Guard vessel had found the wreckage.

I was just buckling into my seat when my cell phone rang. I pulled it out of my pocket and checked the call display.

Malcolm.

I stared at it for a few seconds and knew I couldn't possibly talk to him now when we were about to lift off the ground. So I ignored the call. I slipped the phone back into my pocket and finished buckling in.

Ten seconds later, as I was reaching for my headset, I caught Gary looking at me. "Did you need to take that?" he asked.

"No. It can wait."

"You sure?"

I felt my phone buzz in my pocket, and wondered if it might be an emergency. Quickly, I decided to check it before I switched to airplane mode.

Again, it was Malcolm. This time, he was attempting to reach me by text.

I just tried to call you. You must be busy. Maybe we can talk later, but I think you're right. It's time we took a break. I just had to get that off my chest so that we're clear. No hard feelings. And you don't need to call if you don't want to. I'll understand. Take care of yourself.

As I read Malcolm's message—which was so like him, to be completely unemotional and direct—I felt a sudden twinge of sadness. Was this truly our last good-bye? It seemed so final...so strangely uneventful, considering he had been such a big part of my life for so many years.

Not that I wanted it to be dramatic or hysteric. It wasn't as if I had any reason to be angry with him—unlike my break-up with Kyle, who had behaved like a lunatic caveman.

I couldn't possibly resent Malcolm in any way because I was the one who had suggested the break-up in the first place. He hadn't cheated on me or mistreated me. We were simply caught in a rut and we hadn't even realized it.

For that reason, it was time to go our separate ways. Life was like that sometimes. We change and we grow.

Taking a deep breath, and not feeling entirely certain about what I should say, I texted him back.

Ok.

I stared at my phone for a moment.

I considered typing something more. Surely this warranted a more personal response.

I started to type *I hope we can still be friends*, but I deleted it, because that sounded cliché.

I stared at my screen for a few seconds, and finally added:

It's all good, Malcolm. I appreciate the text. You've never been one to mince words and I appreciate that. You're a good man and you will always hold a special place in my heart. And I'm happy to hear you say that there are no hard feelings. I feel the same. Take care and keep in touch.

I pressed send, knowing in my heart that this was the right thing to do, because I didn't want to live out the rest of my life in such a state of indifference. Not when it came to my romantic relationships. I wanted more than that from the man I loved and who was supposed to love me.

Finally, I switched my phone to airplane mode and slipped it back into my pocket.

A few minutes later, when the chopper lifted off the ground, I was surprised that I felt no anxiety whatsoever. I didn't realize it until we were away from the airport, flying over the water. That's when I realized I had been thinking of other things—like what was possible in my future, which was suddenly wide open before me.

Vacations, maybe?

Sandy beaches and sundresses.

Laughter.

Relaxation.

Passion.

Love.

And every other thing that made life worth living.

Jack

Katelyn clung to me, squeezing fistfuls of my shirt in her hands. "What if he doesn't make it? I don't know what I'll do."

"He'll make it," I said, even though it was a promise I had no business making, because I had no control over what was happening in that trauma room, nor did I have the slightest clue how badly Aaron had been injured. All I knew was that Katelyn needed to hear those words and I wanted to take away her pain.

She stepped back, out of my arms, and I realized other people in the waiting room were staring at us. The last thing I wanted was for this to end up on YouTube.

Taking hold of Katelyn's hand, I made a move to lead her out of there, somewhere more private, when I noticed a bearded man rise from his chair and follow us as we passed. He was wet, as if he'd just come out of the rain, but it wasn't raining outside. He wore faded blue jeans and a navy windbreaker and appeared to be in his early fifties.

I was about to turn around and ask him to back off, to please allow us some privacy, but Katelyn turned also.

"Vince." She broke away from me and walked toward the man, led him to a private space we claimed in a nearby corridor. "Thank God you were with him." She took hold of the man's hand. "My God, look at you. You're soaking wet. Are you all right? What happened?"

Vince nodded at me, and only then did Katelyn realize that we had never met before.

"I'm sorry. Vince, this is my brother-in-law, Jack Peterson. Jack, this is Vince. He works closely with Aaron at the factory."

We shook hands. "It's nice to meet you," Vince said. Then he turned his attention back to Katelyn. "Have you seen him yet?"

"No," she replied. "They won't let us in. I don't even know what happened to him. Can you tell me?"

Vince regarded her with a look of regret. "He took a bad hit, kiddo. That speedboat came at us like a torpedo. It broke a giant hole in the hull. The boat's gone."

"It sank?" Katelyn asked, taking in the enormity of the situation, then shaking her head as if to clear it. "But I don't care about that. I just want to know what happened to Aaron. You said he was distracted."

Vince nodded. "Yes, ma'am. He was having a rough time today, even before this happened." Vince glanced around to make sure no one was listening, and lowered his voice. "We were working with the Coast Guard, fishing out small pieces of floating debris, bagging everything and labeling it to deliver to the investigators, when Aaron spotted something more substantial than a scrap of metal. We both had a bad feeling as we motored closer, and sure enough, it was what we thought."

Vince paused and looked down at his feet. "It was a

little girl with curly blond hair. She couldn't have been more than three."

Katelyn covered her mouth with her hand. "Oh, no."

"We were surprised to find her all in one piece without a single cut or bruise. Aaron leaned over the side to grab hold of her by the shirt collar and lift her aboard. I don't want to go into too much detail, but when he looked down at her face, I think he saw the faces of his own kids, Katelyn, and he lost it. He completely lost it." Vince bowed his head.

"We'd both seen a lot of bad stuff over the past few days, but this was… It was tough on both of us." Vince's eyes lifted. "Aaron cradled that little girl in his arms and he wept with a despair I've never seen in another human being, not in all my God-given days."

Katelyn covered her face with both hands and sank onto a chair, shaking with quiet sobs.

Vince sat down beside her. He put an arm around her to offer some comfort, while I just stood there, imagining my brother holding that little girl in his arms. I knew the feeling. I had seen a child, too, and a battered teddy bear…

Katelyn looked up. Her cheeks were wet with tears. "Is that why he was so distracted?"

Vince nodded. "He was on his knees, rocking that little toddler in his arms when the speedboat came out of nowhere. I turned around at the last second and had a chance to grab onto something, but Aaron didn't see a thing until it was too late. They rammed us on the port side and Aaron and the girl were catapulted up into the air. He struck his head on the way down, on the side of our boat as it was tipping over. He landed in the water. I dove in to get him, but I got tangled up in the rigging and I thought for sure we were both goners. The only blessing was that there were enough rescue boats around to come and help us out. People were diving in, left, right and center. They pulled us aboard a fast little cruiser that took us over to the Coast Guard vessel where a chopper flew us here."

"Thank God," Katelyn said. "Was Aaron conscious at all?"

Vince hesitated, then shook his head. "It wasn't good, Katelyn. They had to do CPR when they pulled him out of the water."

She blinked a few times. "He wasn't breathing?"

"No, but they got him back. I swear, I met some amazing heroes today. We were as lucky as two men can be."

It was my turn, then, to sink onto a chair and comprehend everything Vince had just described. I thought of Aaron, the brother I'd always resented, grieving so deeply for the death of that child.

I thought also of the day I woke up in the hospital in Germany, and he had been there, at my side.

I had made some effort over the years to forget about the past—for the sake of my nieces and nephews, and Katelyn—but it was only a surface forgiveness. Deep down, I still clung to grudges and age-old conflicts.

I realized suddenly that I had not called Aaron to try and connect with him the day before, as I had promised Katelyn I would.

I wished, in that moment, that I had kept my promise. Because how many second chances could one man possibly be given?

Meg

By late afternoon, Gary and I were settled on board a Coast Guard vessel approximately twelve miles east of Kennebunkport, watching a row of video monitors.

A submersible remote control camera had been sent down to the murky depths where the wreckage had been found. With bated breath, we watched the screens as the camera lights illuminated the sandy bottom of the ocean, now a somber, lonely graveyard for what remained of BSA Flight 555.

Fish swam about, curious perhaps.

It wasn't easy to behold the evidence of all those lost lives—broken pieces of luggage, a woman's shoe, a busted laptop, a pair of white plastic sunglasses.

And body parts.

I swallowed uneasily and turned my face away for a moment, then forced myself to focus on what I could make out of the aircraft.

"There she is," Gary said, pointing at the tail, which was painted with a cartoonish image of fluffy white clouds against a turquoise sky—the recognizable logo of Jaeger-Woodrow Airways.

I sat forward in my seat. "There's not much left of it, but at least it's something." I pointed. "Look, there. The way the metal is twisted. That's likely where the explosion occurred, on the port side, to the rear of the cargo hold." I turned to Gary. "We're definitely going to have to bring her up, and every piece of her that we can get our hands on down there."

The camera continued to cruise along the length of the hull, shining its light on the exterior.

"Can you get some footage of the inside?" I asked, pointing again. "Go in right there. Yes. Good. Now can you turn the camera to the right?" I squinted to try and get a better perspective on the damage.

"Do you see what I see?" Gary asked.

"Yes," I replied. "Look at that molten metal. There must have been a fire before the explosion, but what caused it? And why didn't the pilots notify air traffic control? Were the smoke detectors not working?"

"We should know something about that fairly soon," Gary said, "now that we have the CVR." He checked his watch. "They're probably listening to the cockpit recordings this very minute."

"In the meantime, let's keep looking," I said. "It's a pretty large debris field down there. Can we go explore a bit, just follow the wreckage."

The tech guy maneuvered the camera to travel along the sandy field of mangled metal and scorched electrical wires. We passed a few more busted laptops, and more burned up rubble from the cargo hold—suitcases, shampoo bottles and all sorts of devices like tablets and cell phones.

Then all at once, the beam of light from the camera illuminated what appeared to be a wide, dense field of shiny silver objects, gleaming as the light passed over them.

"Oh my God. Do you see that?" I asked Gary as I bent forward and inclined my head. "What the heck? No way."

Gary removed his glasses and bent to peer more closely at the screen. "No, that can't be," he said. "There are thousands of them."

We stared at the screen while the camera panned from left to right and floated over a dense expanse of lithium-ion batteries of all types and sizes. There were button batteries, 9-Volt batteries, double and triple A's, rechargeable battery boxes… Some were shiny and new, while others were black and burned.

Each one had the company logo *Oxy-GeoTech* emblazoned on the surface, and there was no sign of any protective packaging. Not that it mattered. With or without packaging, the air transfer of lithium batteries for further sale or distribution was strictly prohibited by the FAA.

"If this is what it looks like," I said, "and Jaeger-Woodrow Airways is shipping these things in the cargo hold, they're going to be in a lot of trouble."

"You're telling me."

Gary picked up a phone and called headquarters.

CHAPTER

Thirty-nine

Jack

Katelyn and I had been sitting at Aaron's bedside in the ICU for five hours straight when she rose from her chair, squirming.

"I can't hold it anymore," she said. "I have to go to the bathroom, but I don't want to leave him. I want to be here if…*when* he wakes up."

I recognized an undertone—that she didn't want to be gone from the room if something else happened.

"I'll be right here," I told her, rising to move to the chair she had been occupying, closer to the head of the bed.

"I'll be quick," she said. "If he wakes up, tell him I'm here."

"I will."

She hurried from the room.

All I could do was sit and listen to the sound of her anxious footfalls, beating quickly down the hall to the nearest washroom. Then there was only silence, except for the steady beeping of the heart monitor.

I looked down at my brother's pale, still face behind the oxygen mask and was struck by my keen awareness of

Katelyn's unconditional love for him and his love for her. There was a permanence between the two. Something unbreakable and eternal that would continue beyond this life and this world.

It was a glimpse at something I had never truly considered before now—that Katelyn had found it in herself to forgive all imperfections and petty arguments and whatever else might have stood in the way of their undying devotion to each other.

I felt suddenly inadequate, because I had never known such a forgiving love.

Aaron wasn't perfect. She knew it as well as anyone because he had, in the past, fallen from grace, as we all have at one time or another. He had been unfaithful to her. On that day, when she learned of it, I tried to convince her to choose me over him, but instead she had chosen to forgive.

I had walked away from them, putting distance between us, while resenting Aaron for his triumph, which was undeserved, in my mind.

As far as my brother was concerned, I could never think of anything but his missteps, and how it was unjust that he always won, in spite of them.

But wasn't it true that sometimes, the most important lessons are learned from our most regrettable mistakes? He had said that once—that regret is a powerful teacher.

Katelyn had forgiven him eons ago, and look at them now? Aaron was a good man with a good heart, as loyal as they came. There was no doubt in my mind that they would be together forever, more deeply devoted to each other than anyone I'd ever known.

I couldn't deny a momentary flash of jealousy. Not

because I wanted Katelyn for myself. What I wanted was *what* they had.

Love. Unconditional love. The permanent, soulful connection that could never be severed, not even under the most dire circumstances, including death.

Aaron and I had grown up together, for better or worse. As children, we started out on a rocky path with a dark history. But maybe we had been placed on this earth as brothers for a reason.

Maybe this time, I was the one with lessons to learn.

Katelyn returned to the room just then, and I stood up to give her chair back to her. As I watched her take hold of Aaron's hand, I prayed that he would come back to us, because for the first time, I felt as if my fate with my brother was not sealed, that the past did not dictate the future. Every day was a new day, a new opportunity to start fresh. Intellectually, I'd always known that, but why had I never been able to apply it to my relationship with Aaron?

My cell phone rang, and I saw that it was Meg. I left the room to answer it. "Hello?"

"Hi, Jack." Just the sound of her voice was a comfort to me. "I heard about your brother. It was on the news. Are you okay?"

I leaned against the wall and tipped my head back. "He's not doing so well."

Meg was quiet for a moment. "I'm sorry. Is there anything I can do? Would you like me to come over there?"

I pushed away from the wall and walked slowly toward the visitors lounge. "No, we're all right. I'm here with Katelyn, and my parents are on their way. Besides, I imagine you've got your hands full. I heard they found the black box earlier today."

"That's right," she replied.

I glanced at the clerk at the nurses' station as I passed by. "What's going on with that?"

She sighed. "Do you really want to hear this?"

"Yeah, I could use a distraction."

"Well. We're still waiting for the data from the black box, but I just got back from the Coast Guard vessel where they found the rest of the wreckage. There's going to be some news about that at the press conference tonight. Are you planning to be there?"

I walked into the lounge and sat down on a sofa. "No, I called my producer to get Joe to take over for me and do my show tonight. I just need..." I paused. "I need to be here right now."

"Of course." Meg hesitated. "Listen, Jack...I've never met your brother, but...I wish I could be there with you... Just to be there."

We were both quiet, and I swallowed over a thick lump that rose up in my throat.

"Can you tell me what I'll be missing at the press conference?" I asked, because I knew that if I started talking about Aaron, I might not be able to keep it together.

Meg cleared her throat. "I probably shouldn't reveal this yet, but the whole world is going to know pretty soon anyway." She paused again. "There were some developments this afternoon. We can't say for sure if this is what caused the explosion—we'll need to bring up the wreckage and do a formal examination of the damage to the plane—but when we sent a camera down to film what was on the ocean floor, we found something we didn't expect to see."

I frowned. "What was it?"

"Brace yourself." She sighed with a note of defeat. "There were thousands of lithium-ion batteries down there. You wouldn't have believed it. I've never seen anything like it. It was like a giant field of shiny, silver grass."

I pressed my hand to my forehead in disbelief. "You're kidding me. That's breaking a few rules, isn't it?"

"Yes. Everyone in the aviation world knows that lithium batteries are strictly prohibited in the cargo holds of aircrafts because they can combust. I can't even begin to comprehend their blatant and totally careless disregard for FAA rules and regulations."

"How in the world could that have happened?" I asked.

"We're still trying to figure it out. What we do know is that the battery shipment wasn't listed with the airline, so someone was obviously getting around security, sneaking it on somehow. The FBI and our team at the airport are looking into it now, interviewing the airline employees, baggage handlers, and everyone else who played a part in getting that flight off the ground. They'll get to the bottom of it, I swear it on my life. But either way, Reg Harrison has a lot to answer for, because guess what company manufactured those batteries?"

I sat forward. "Please, tell me it wasn't Oxy-GeoTech."

"Bingo."

I sat back and let out a breath. "That man needs to go to jail."

"I agree. But listen, I have to get going. We have a team briefing before the press conference and I have to make a few calls about the black box. But will you call me or text me later about your brother? I'll be thinking about you, Jack, and saying prayers."

I felt a wave of calm move over me, and a strong desire

to be with her again. "Thank you Meg. I'll be thinking about you, too. Good luck tonight."

We hung up and I returned to Aaron's room in the ICU.

When I entered, I found Katelyn in tears. My stomach dropped.

"Is everything okay?" I asked.

She turned to me. "I don't know. Why won't he wake up, Jack? What will I do if he doesn't?"

Meg

I t was nearly midnight when I finally slid my key card into the lock of my hotel room and pushed the door open. I couldn't wait to get into my pajamas and brush my teeth—maybe pour a glass of wine from the minibar—because it had been that kind of day.

The press conference that evening was pure pandemonium after Gary and I revealed what we'd seen at the bottom of the Atlantic. Questions were asked: How was it possible that a major commercial airliner, taking off from a major U.S. airport, had managed to get a shipment of potentially explosive, restricted materials into the cargo hold? Was no one paying attention? Was no one doing their job? There were nearly two hundred souls on board that doomed flight. Innocent passengers. Mothers, sons, daughters, husbands. How could this have happened?

I had no explanation for those who wanted answers, and it was probably the most trying, discouraging moment of my career—to face the family members and tell them what we still *didn't* know.

The investigation was far from over, and we would need

to examine all the evidence to determine what exactly caused the plane to crash, but no matter what we concluded in the coming weeks and months, it was impossible to reverse what had occurred. The end result would be the same. A plane had crashed and innocent people had died.

I closed my hotel room door, locked it, and flopped onto my back on the bed. I felt numb all over. Disturbed and full of grief.

Staring up at the ceiling, I tried to calm my mind and rein in my emotions, and even so, there was something about this particular crash that was hitting me harder than any other.

I was having a difficult time coming to grips with it—maybe because it had been caused by the same man who was negligent in the past and had gotten away with it, scot-free. People died in 1984, including Jack's childhood friend. I didn't want to let that monster get away with it again. Not this time. Not on my watch.

Sitting up, I thought of Jack and his brother in the hospital. I felt an intense longing and wanted desperately to know how they were both doing. So I rose to my feet, withdrew my phone from my jacket pocket and checked my messages.

There were none from Jack, so I decided to text him as I crossed to the minibar.

Hey. How are you?

I pressed send, set the phone down on the top of the fridge and went to change into my pajamas. A few minutes later, I returned to the fridge and opened it up. Inside, I found two small bottles of Pinot Grigio, among other things.

Ah, yes. This was exactly what I needed.

I unscrewed one cap and poured it into a glass. I was just taking the first sip when my phone buzzed. I reached to pick it up.

I've been better, Jack replied. *Aaron is still the same. I'm just leaving the hospital now. How are you?*

I could feel his despair almost physically, so I was quick to respond.

I had a rough day, too. Just poured myself a glass of wine out of the minibar. Would you like one? If so, I'm in room 621.

My phone vibrated almost instantly, and my heart skipped a beat.

You sure? Because I could use a glass of wine. I could be there in about ten minutes.

I quickly thumbed a response. *Yes. Please come. I want to see you.*

There was so much to talk about, and not just what was going on with his brother and the latest developments in the investigation. I wanted to talk about other things too—the highs and lows of his life. I felt a yearning for him—to truly *know* everything about him—and the intensity of that desire baffled me.

Another text came in. *Ok. See you shortly.*

Excitement flooded my veins. I hurried to brush my teeth and pull on a light sweater.

~♂

Five minutes later, I opened my door to find Jack standing in the hall, looking impossibly gorgeous in blue jeans and a red plaid shirt. But there were dark circles under his eyes and his hair was tousled, as if he'd been raking his fingers through it all day. How weary he looked.

I stepped aside and invited him in.

"I'm sorry about this," he said as I quietly closed the door behind him. "It's late, and I see you're in your pajamas. Are you sure this is okay?"

"Of course," I replied. "I wanted to see you."

His shoulders rose and fell with a deep intake of breath, and when he gazed across at me with unadulterated sorrow, all I wanted to do was take away his pain.

Stepping forward, I said, "Come here." I pulled him into my arms where we stood for a long time without speaking, simply embracing each other.

It felt good—*more* than good—to run my hand up and down his back and to lay my cheek on his shoulder. I felt the stroke of his fingers slide up under my hair to cup the back of my neck, and I wanted to stay like that forever.

When we stepped apart, he said in a low, meaningful voice, "Thank you."

I nodded and took him by the hand to lead him away from the door. "Red or white?" I gestured toward the minibar. "I have both. There's Merlot and Pinot Grigio, plus a few little bottles of vodka and gin.

"I'll take the Merlot," he replied.

I poured him a glass and he moved to sit down in the chair by the window. The drapes were closed. "What a day."

I sat down in the chair facing him. "Still no change?"

Jack shook his head and sipped his wine. "No. It's a head trauma, which they say is unpredictable. He could wake up in five minutes, or not at all. Ever. Katelyn's taking it pretty hard. Those two are like…" He paused. "I don't know how to describe it. I don't think a word exists for what they have. 'Love' doesn't even capture it."

I leaned back in my chair. "They were lucky to have

found each other." Looking down at the wine in my glass, I swirled it about. "I don't think I've ever loved anyone like that."

"Not even Malcolm?"

I pursed my lips at him and shook my head. "No. And that's over now. I'm embarrassed to say we ended it by text message this morning—which is actually not surprising when I think about it, considering how totally uncommitted we were to each other. It wasn't anything like what your brother and his wife must have."

"I'm sorry to hear that," Jack said. "But at the same time, I'm not sorry."

I gave him a flirty look because I could see where he was going with this, and it caused a wonderful thrill in me.

Jack gazed toward the drapes, and became lost in thought.

"You're thinking about your brother," I said.

"Feeling guilty, mostly."

"Why?"

"Because we never got along well in life," he said, meeting my eyes. "I don't know why I couldn't just bury the hatchet when I had the chance."

I blinked a few times. "What happened between you?"

Jack took another sip of his wine and shrugged. "I don't know. It all seems stupid now. But all through our lives, we were in competition with each other and often ended up fighting over the same girl. Aaron seemed to win at everything, and I often felt like his successes were taking something away from me, because he eclipsed me in every way. I just couldn't get out from under his shadow, and there were times when I felt like he actually enjoyed crushing me…as if to get back at me, to keep me in my place."

"Get back at you for what?"

Jack shook his head and looked down at his wine. "It's a long story…about things that go way back. Anyhow, when he married Katelyn, I went away to Afghanistan and…well, you know the rest of the story. I got hit in a roadside bombing and…" Jack sipped his wine as he recalled what happened. "Aaron was the first person to arrive at my bedside."

I said nothing. I simply waited for Jack to explain the rest because I suspected there was much more to the story that what he was telling me.

"Aaron apologized for not letting go of the past and he wanted to start over. I think it shook him up, to see me like that. He saw it as a wake-up call because I almost died, but sadly, it wasn't a wake-up call for me. I suppose, in my defense, I was in a lot of pain and it was hard to see past that. But I just couldn't forgive or forget all the fights we'd had, for all those years. So that's how it stayed. Even after I came home, neither of us talked to each other much."

"And now you find yourself at *his* bedside," I said, "and the roles are reversed."

Jack looked up and frowned. "I feel like we're all being tossed around in the vortex of a cyclone, and it's just tragedy all around us, spinning out of control. It's made me think about a lot of things this past week. Things from my past. And you know what? My brother's not a bad guy. It's like I'm just realizing this now, for the first time, when I refused to see it before. All I saw before was…" He paused. "Stuff from another life. I don't want to do that anymore." Jack met my gaze directly. "Meeting you has helped. I can't say why, but you make me feel somehow… I don't know… Grounded in the present."

I stared at him in the golden lamplight and marveled at the fact that I felt such a comfortable intimacy with him after only a few days of knowing him. I imagined that if we had known each other as children or in high school or college, we would have been lifelong friends.

"Sometimes…" I said, swirling the wine around in my glass, "I think things are meant to happen when they are meant to happen. I think we're supposed to go through life one day at a time, put one foot in front of the other, make a bunch of mistakes and figure things out as we go. Maybe there's a reason it took you this long to learn to forgive your brother. I don't know what that reason is, but maybe it'll be clear to you someday."

Jack regarded me thoughtfully, then he nodded. "I'm constantly amazed by the things in life that still surprise me. Things I learn about myself, and other people. Just when you think you've seen it all…"

I chuckled. "Life never quits being thought provoking and mysterious. It's curious, isn't it? I think I might have to live a few more lives before I get it all figured out." I sipped my wine.

The corner of Jack's mouth curled up in a small grin, and I was glad to have provided him with some amusement when he was so worried about his brother.

"Can you tell me about the press conference tonight?" he asked, sitting forward to rest his elbows on his knees. "How was it for you?"

I let out a breath and finished my wine. "It was rough. You know how passionate I am about my work, and to think that I've devoted the past decade of my life, working around the clock to ensure safety in the skies, and something like this can still happen." I stood up to pour another glass of wine. "We recommend rules for a reason, and the FAA implements them to prevent this kind of thing. Yet still, somehow…"

"I watched the briefing on my phone," Jack said. "You were good, Meg. You were compassionate and clear about everything."

I returned to my chair. "Thank you. But people were still pointing fingers, at the FAA and the airport, for not doing a better job at policing Jaeger-Woodrow and ensuring that security was as tight as it should have been. Think about it—if someone could smuggle a huge shipment of batteries onto a major commercial airliner, why not a terrorist bomb?" I huffed with frustration. "God, it was awful. The anger and fear in the room was palpable, and rightly so. I felt it myself, because I've been an innocent passenger on airplanes numerous times. All you can do is trust that the airlines are doing their jobs and that the statistics will be in your favor during your flight. But at the end of the day, even as an investigator for the NTSB, I can't control what happens every time. No matter how badly I want to."

We sat for a long while, pondering that fact. Then I yawned.

"You're tired. I should go." Jack finished his wine and set the glass down on the small round table between us.

"No, please don't," I replied, shaking my head. "I just want to close my eyes for a few seconds." I stood up and crawled across the bed. I lay down on my side, curled up in a ball, and squeezed the fat feather pillow under my cheek. "You're tired, too," I said. "Come and lie down." Feeling a little tipsy, I patted the empty space on the bed beside me.

Jack crawled onto the bed and joined me.

THE COLOR OF A PROMISE

We lay on our sides, facing each other. I asked him about Aaron again and the women they had fought over. Jack told me that he once fancied himself in love with Aaron's wife, Katelyn, before they were married. This surprised me. Evidently, Katelyn was the main reason they were estranged, and this was why Jack had held on to that feeling of competitiveness toward his brother.

"Do you still love her?" I asked.

Jack shook his head. "No. Not that way. These days, I care about her more like a sister."

"So she's not the great love of your life?"

He shook his head. "No. She's the great love of Aaron's life and I know that now. I have yet to meet the great love of mine."

"Me, too."

We lay for a moment in the lamplight while I studied all the beautiful contours of his face. He was the most handsome man I had ever seen, and I felt hopeful and optimistic.

Happy.

I then told him about my past relationships—or lack of them. I explained how I'd been a nerd in high school and didn't have a boyfriend until my third year in college, when I met a guy who was completely wrong for me.

"Why was he wrong for you?" Jack asked.

"Because he was immature and irresponsible. He liked to party all the time and didn't care about his grades, but for some strange reason I was attracted to him. His name was Kyle. Incidentally, he kind of looked like you," I said with a grin. "Maybe that's why I fell head over heels."

Jack smiled and took the compliment in stride.

I fluffed the pillow under my cheek. "I think 'Wild Kyle'

was the reason I swung like a pendulum in the opposite direction, toward the most responsible guy in the universe, who was not the least bit spontaneous or fun. Malcolm was an enabler, when you think about it. He enabled me to be obsessed with my job and have no life. Now here I am. A single workaholic."

Jack pushed a lock of hair behind my ear, and I felt a delightful shiver of awareness in every part of my body.

"Now you just need to find the right balance," he said, "because you can't live out the rest of your days without having any fun."

"Damn straight," I replied. "Life's too precious and too short. You never know when your number's going to come up."

I closed my eyes, just for a moment.

When I opened them again, a ray of sunlight was beaming through the crack in the hotel drapes, and Jack's cell phone was ringing on the bedside table.

I realized we were entwined in each other's arms. My cheek was resting on his shoulder, my open hand was on the front of his shirt, my leg draped across his muscular, jean-clad thigh.

Groggily, I sat up and checked the clock. It was 6:09 a.m.

"Your phone's ringing," I said, passing it to him as he lifted his head off the pillow.

He checked the call display. All the color drained from his face as he sat up. "It's Katelyn." He glanced at me. "I'm afraid to answer this."

I also sat up and laid my hand on his shoulder.

Jack swiped the screen and raised it to his cheek. "Hey, Katelyn. I'm here. Is everything okay?"

I sucked in a breath and held it, and watched his profile.

Jack's gaze darted to meet mine. My heart nearly burst out of my chest as he reached for my hand.

"He's awake."

Meg

As soon as Jack left for the hospital, I grabbed a quick shower and hustled downstairs to the hotel conference room for a 7:00 a.m. meeting. Gary had texted to let me know that we'd finally received the data from the black box.

The flight data indicated that the plane had been in the air for twenty-one minutes after takeoff. It had reached a cruising altitude of 30,000 feet, and was on the proper course when there was a sudden and complete loss of power and the plane disappeared from radar. All the communications radios and transponders went dead at precisely the same second, so there was very little to go on after that.

Similarly, the cockpit voice recorder revealed nothing of help to us. There were no distress calls from the pilots, nor did any members of the cabin crew knock on the cockpit door to alert the pilots of a fire anywhere on board. No one smelled smoke or reported any equipment failures. Everything simply went dead, which could only mean that there was an explosion of massive proportions, to have caused such total, instantaneous loss of power.

But still, we could not presume that the lithium batteries had caused the explosion until we examined all the evidence more closely. It was clear to me that I would have to reconstruct the cargo hold in order to see the effects of the blast, and we would continue looking for evidence of a bomb. Its effects could merely have been proliferated by the batteries in the hold. At this point, I wasn't ruling out anything.

When we finished our meeting, I checked my phone for messages as I headed out of the hotel to return to the hangar. A text had just come in from Jack.

Thank you for last night. Things are good here. Aaron is awake and doing well. Call me when you can.

I breathed a sigh of relief and dialed his number.

~*O*~

Jack and I saw each other again that night in my hotel room, after a long day of work in the hangar and another press briefing. We both knew it would be our last night together for a while, for he had to fly back to New York the following day and return to the studio.

We stayed up until 3:00 in the morning, discussing the latest developments in the investigation, but mostly talking about the blessing of Aaron's recovery. Jack told me how they had spoken at length about a number of issues from the past, including Jack's heartbreak and anger over his first love, Jeannie Morrison, who wound up in a closet making out with Aaron at a middle school party. Jack and Aaron agreed to start over as brothers and put all past conflicts behind them.

When Jack left my room in the wee hours of the

morning, he kissed me passionately, then touched his forehead to mine and held my face in his hands as he made a promise—that he would return to Cape Elizabeth to be with me again as soon as possible. He also promised to call every day.

When the time came for him to walk out my door, neither of us wanted to let go.

Over the following week, he kept his promise and called every day—sometimes more than once. We talked for hours when I returned to my hotel room each night.

Gary was both pleased and surprised when I quit for the day at the same time he did, rather than working overtime until I couldn't keep my eyes open. Gary was a family man, and he believed we should all have a life outside of work. I was beginning to see the importance of that, because life was indeed precious. How could I not have grasped that reality before now, considering what I did for a living?

I reminded myself that everything happens in due time. We learn the lessons we are meant to learn when the moment is right.

The following weekend, Jack surprised me by showing up at my hotel with flowers and a dinner invitation—from his brother, Aaron, and his sister-in-law, Katelyn. They both wanted to meet me.

We all spent the evening at their penthouse condo, with their children as well, talking and laughing around the dinner table, eating great food and drinking wine.

Sadly, Jack had to leave the next morning to return to New York. Again, he promised to call every day. He kept his promise, and we grew closer with every moment while I continued my work on the investigation.

At long last, everyone's scrupulous dedication finally paid off. Not long after they brought the tail up from the deep, I received a phone call about another shocking discovery.

Forty-two

Meg

"You're not going to believe what else they found down there," Gary said. He had called me from his car and on his way to the hangar where I had been working since 7:00 a.m. "They were lucky to have stumbled on it, about 200 yards from where the tail landed on the ocean floor. They're bringing it up now."

I strode into the office at the hangar and closed the door to block out the sound of a noisy hammer pounding against metal. "Don't keep me in suspense, Gary. What is it?"

"They found an oxygen tank with a broken seal—the kind they use for medical purposes. I'm sure it won't surprise you to hear what logo was printed on the side."

"Oxy-GeoTech," I replied. I sank into a chair and pinched the bridge of my nose. "But maybe it was an empty canister? Do we know?"

"It looks to be empty right now, but based on what I'm seeing, it was probably full when it was placed on board because there was plastic packing tape over the seal."

"Packing tape!" I replied with horror. "An oxygen tank in a cargo hold, sealed with packing tape… That airline knows no bounds."

"Apparently not."

"Did they only find the one?"

"So far, but they're still searching. There could be more, and we're talking to all the employees."

"Good. Keep me posted. I gotta go."

We hung up and I awaited the arrival of the tank, which I knew was going to be an important puzzle piece.

~ 0

Over the next week, the full picture became clear. Three more tanks were discovered on the ocean floor and they were searching for more.

With my painstaking reconstruction of the blast area in the cargo hold, the careful analysis of the materials by explosive experts, and the honest testimonies of workers at the airport, we were able to confirm that an initial fire had been caused by the illegally stored lithium batteries, which had spontaneously ignited. Under normal circumstances, the fire might have blown itself out, but with the presence of the loose oxygen tanks in the cargo hold—which hadn't been stowed properly and leaked after being knocked around—a massive explosion had occurred and blown the aircraft to pieces.

I was so infuriated by the discovery—and the fact that history had indeed repeated itself—that I asked for permission to accompany the FBI agents when they entered Reginald Harrison's corporate office in Washington. He was to be arrested under multiple charges of criminal negligence related to his airline. On top of that, he was being nailed for tax evasion.

It was by far the most satisfying moment of my career when I watched the FBI agents slap cuffs on him in his luxurious corner office on the twenty-first floor of his glass tower, and drag him out of the building while photographers snapped pictures.

In that moment, the decade-worth of stress and anxiety I had suffered was completely worth it. I had not one single regret.

~ ⊘

That evening, Jack reported Reg Harrison's arrest with class, accuracy and precision. I was glued to the television screen like never before, and Jack seemed a hero to me as he spoke about the 1984 disaster as well as the details of Flight 555, along with mention of Reg Harrison's numerous other breaches of ethics as a business man.

Of course, I was head over heels in love with Jack at that point, but when I found myself weeping tears of joy and satisfaction at his commentary, I knew there would never be any man in the world more special to me. I believed in my heart that he was destined to be the great love of my life, and even after a mere few weeks of knowing him, I would have married him that day if he had asked. That's how certain I was that he was the one for me. The only one.

When his show ended, I texted him.

Great job tonight. You're my hero.

He replied immediately. *I was just reporting the facts. If anyone is a hero today, it's you. Congratulations on a job well done.*

As soon as I read his words, I burst into tears. When my phone rang a few minutes later and I saw that it was him, I wiped my eyes and answered.

"I just realized something," Jack said, without preamble.

"What's that?"

"I've never met your parents, and you've never met mine."

I chuckled softly. "That's an interesting observation. Is there a reason you're telling me this now?"

He paused, and I imagined him sitting down on a chair in his dressing room, loosening his tie. "Yes. Tomorrow's Sunday and I have the day off. My parents are back in Chicago and my mother is on my case about meeting you. So I was wondering if you might like to join me and my family in the windy city for lunch."

"That's a bit of a commute," I replied, "considering you're in New York, I'm still in Portland, and lunch will be served halfway across the country."

"You are correct," he said, "but where there's a will there's a way. I could pick you, Katelyn, Aaron and the kids up in my private jet first thing in the morning, and we'd be there by ten. Then I could send the jet to pick up your parents in Boise and bring them to Chicago in time for a late lunch. How does that sound?"

I felt my eyebrows fly up. "That sounds lovely. I'll have to check with my parents first to make sure they're available. But I don't think you ever mentioned this to me before, Jack. You have your own jet?"

He paused. "Is that going to be a problem? Because I know you're not crazy about flying."

I laughed. "I'll be fine."

"All right then," he replied. "I'll pick you up at nine, and I'm looking forward to spending the day together."

"Me, too," I said affectionately. "I can't wait to see where you grew up."

Neither of us said anything for a moment, and I felt positively blissful.

"I'll see you in the morning," Jack said.

I smiled. "I can hardly wait."

CHAPTER

Forty-three

Jack

She was at the airport, waiting for me when I landed. Dressed in a blue floral sundress and flat sparkly sandals, with her blond hair pulled back in a high ponytail, she took my breath away as she crossed the tarmac.

"It's good to see you," I said to her as she climbed the gangway steps and came on board. I pulled her into my arms and held her. She smelled like lavender, and I wanted to devour her whole. "I missed you."

"I missed you, too," she replied, burying her face in my neck. "I'm so glad you're here." She stepped back. "But I haven't seen Aaron and Katelyn yet."

"They're on their way." I took hold of her hand and led her into the main cabin.

"Wow," she said, taking in the white leather seats and polished wood paneling. "You like to travel in style."

Grace, my regular flight attendant, appeared out of the rear galley with a silver tray, carrying two glasses of champagne and orange juice and a bowl of fresh strawberries.

"This is Grace," I said. "She's been with me for six

years. She just happens to be married to the captain, so they're a great team."

"How nice." Meg peered toward the cockpit where the pilot and co-pilot were going over their final instrument checks. "It's a pleasure to meet you, Grace."

Grace set the strawberries down on the low table in front of us. "It's a pleasure to meet you, too," she said. "Please make yourself comfortable. We're just waiting for the others to arrive, and then we'll be underway."

"Thank you," Meg replied, giving me a look. "I feel like Cinderella," she whispered when Grace returned to the galley.

I laughed. "I don't mind as long I get to be the prince."

Meg raised her glass and clinked it with mine. "Deal."

A few minutes later, Aaron, Katelyn and the children climbed the gangway steps in a flurry of laughter and excitement.

Aaron was the last person to step on board. He paused just inside the door, looking around. "Wow. This is the first time I've been on your jet, Jack. Pretty impressive. Well done."

"It comes in handy on occasion," I replied. "We'll have to start putting it to better use. Take some trips. All of us. Together."

He and I exchanged a look that could only be described as a shared contentment. "That sounds like a plan I can get behind."

Aaron smiled at Meg. "Hey, Meg. It's good to see you."

"It's good to see you, too," she replied with warmth.

Then Aaron strode forward and gave my shoulder a squeeze as he moved to help Katelyn settle the children in their seats.

~*Ø*

An hour later, I arranged for two separate cars to pick us up at the Chicago airport and drive us to my parents' home.

As Meg and I entered the suburban neighborhood where I grew up, I asked our driver to take a left instead of following Aaron's car to the right. We would still end up at the same place because the street formed a loop, but I wanted to drive past Millicent's house.

"That's where my friend Gordon used to live," I told Meg as we drove past his old house.

Meg leaned forward to take a look. "It's pretty." She commented on the lush green ivy that covered the trellis at the front gate. Then she turned to me. "So where was the infamous party at Mark Hennigar's, where your first love ended up in the closet with Aaron? Was that near here?"

"Mark's house is just around the corner," I said with a chuckle. "We'll drive past it in a second or two."

I pointed it out, and Meg was quiet as we drove by, simply gazing out the window, taking it all in.

A moment later, I leaned across the seat and pointed. "That was the Davenport house, where my friend Millicent lived." We drove by slowly. Meg took a long look at the brick colonial architecture, the wide green lawn, and the colorful garden.

I watched her intently, wishing I could see her face, but all I could see was the back of her head.

She turned to me. "It's exactly how I pictured it. And it's a shame…what happened to them. But I'm glad we finally nailed Harrison, and that he's behind bars where he belongs. That feels good, doesn't it?"

"It certainly does," I replied.

Meg sat back in her seat and faced forward. She folded her hands on her lap and said nothing more.

Well, then…

Obviously, Katelyn had been right when she spoke to me weeks ago in the hotel ballroom, just before one of the press briefings. She had pushed me to stop trying to find meaning, connections and relevance in the past, and simply live *this* life.

It was clear to me now that Meg had no memory of any past lives, and it didn't matter anyway. Maybe she was Millicent; maybe she wasn't. Either way, I loved her. She was the most incredible woman I'd ever met.

A few minutes later, we pulled up in front of my parents' modest home and got out of the car. She studied the front of it and smiled at me.

God, she was dazzling. Those blue eyes knocked the wind right out of me, because I saw the future in them.

I wanted to marry her—right then and there.

~ ❧

Meg's parents arrived shortly after noon.

Meg hadn't seen her parents in over three months, and we all enjoyed meeting each other and hugging in my parents' small entrance hall. There was much laughter and gushing. Mrs. Andrews brought wine and a box of homemade brownies. My mother was delighted.

They served braised ham, potato salad, and steamed asparagus for lunch in our formal dining room.

It was the perfect environment to get better acquainted. Our parents discovered they had a great deal in common. Like my own father, Meg's father enjoyed fishing, as did Aaron, so they all had plenty to talk about. In addition, Meg's mother was an avid cook, and so our moms compared recipes and discussed all their favorite cooking shows on television, while Meg and Katelyn helped serve dessert and coffee.

Eventually, the conversation turned to the latest developments with the crash investigation, and Meg explained that it would be awhile before they could publish their official accident report, and Harrison's trial would take time in court as well.

Meg laid her hand on my knee under the table. "It was satisfying to discover the cause of the crash, no doubt about it," she said, "but at the same time, I never feel much like celebrating, because nothing can bring back all those poor people who died, and nothing can take away the pain of the families—not even a lifetime sentence for Reg Harrison." She picked up her coffee cup and took a sip. "On that note…" She regarded her parents, directly across the table. "You're probably going to shoot me for this, but I think…I might want to make a career change."

Her father frowned.

"What kind of change?" her mother asked, setting down her dessert fork and looking surprised.

I glanced at my father, who sat at the head of the table, and shrugged, because I had no idea what she was about to say.

Meg set down her cup. "Of course I'm going to finish this accident case and file the report, but after that…" She paused and cleared her throat. "I think I might want to leave my job at the NTSB."

A hush fell over the room. Even I was dumbfounded because this was the first I'd heard of it. Meg had told me about her desire to take more vacation time, and I'd seen firsthand the stress and anxiety she suffered because of her work, but she had never talked about leaving her job.

Yet, I was not surprised.

"But you've worked so hard to get where you are," her father said. "And college wasn't cheap. What are you thinking about doing, baby? Something in the engineering field, I hope?"

Meg looked down at her dessert plate and poked at her apple crisp where the ice cream was melting. "I don't know," she said. "You'll probably think I'm nuts, but I might like to go back to school. Maybe study architecture. I've always wanted to build houses. I think I'd be really good at it."

Something in me lurched at her confession, and I leaned back, staring at her profile with fascination as I rested my arm along the back of her chair.

Her father sat back as well and nodded at her. "I'm sure you would be *very* good at it, dear. You're always good at whatever you set your mind to. So if that's what you want to do, then you should go for it. Life's too short. Do what makes you happy. We'll support you any way we can."

She smiled at him. "I haven't made my mind up for sure yet," she said. "It's a big decision. But thanks for understanding."

Mr. Andrews raised his glass. "To new beginnings."

We all toasted to that, and talked about the Chicago Bears while we finished our desserts.

Later, after Meg and Katelyn helped my mother tidy up in the kitchen, I found Meg in the hallway, pulled her close, and whispered in her ear. "Would you like to steal a few minutes to be alone? Take a walk with me?"

"I'd love that," she replied.

A few minutes later, we left our families on the back

deck while the children played in the yard, and snuck out the front door.

"It's the weirdest thing," Meg said as we walked hand in hand up the street. "I've been having these intense feelings of *déjà vu* all day long, ever since we got here."

I felt a strange buzzing in my ears, maybe because of my sudden pounding pulse. "Does that happen to you often?"

"No," she said. "I mean, sometimes… But not like this."

I squeezed her hand. "What feels familiar? Anything specific?"

"I don't know. I can't really put my finger on it. But there's something about this neighborhood. I feel like I've been here before, or maybe I dreamed about it."

We walked leisurely, and she stopped to smell some fall roses at a neighbor's gate.

"I always kind of enjoy being hit with a spell of *déjà vu*," I told her. "It makes me curious."

"Yes," she replied. "It's one of those mysteries in life. It feels kind of magical."

We continued walking until we arrived at a groomed path that led to the wooded area behind Millicent's old house. I turned onto it.

"We used to play here," I said, "when we were kids. We built a stone bridge across the creek and started to build a fort. Or a 'clubhouse,' as Millicent preferred to call it. We earned the supplies by doing chores for her father."

"You *started* a clubhouse… Did you ever finish it?" Meg asked as we walked deeper into the shady forest.

"No, we didn't have the chance. We only got the first wall constructed before Millicent left for Arizona and never came back."

A mourning dove cooed in the trees, somewhere in the distance, and I heard the familiar sound of rushing water in the creek.

When we came to it, Meg was first to make her way gingerly across the stone bridge, leaping from one moss-covered rock to another to avoid getting splashed by the rushing water.

"It still works," she said happily, spreading her arms wide as she reached the other side. "Come on!"

Mesmerized by how joyful she was, I followed. When I reached her—not having regained my balance yet—she pulled me close and kissed me hard.

"I think you're my dream girl," I said.

She smiled, grabbed hold of my hand and led me deeper into the woods, in the direction of the clubhouse we had begun a lifetime ago.

We?

Stop it, Jack.

Working to stay grounded in the present, I paused and looked around. Suddenly I grew concerned that I wouldn't remember where we'd begun construction, because nothing looked familiar. On top of that, I had no idea if there would be anything left of it. All we'd managed to build all those years ago was one wall, with planks nailed horizontally to a couple of tree trunks. Someone might have come along and scavenged the wood in the past thirty years, or completed the structure, for all I knew.

Oddly, Meg led the way. All I could do was hold her hand and follow.

"Is that it?" she asked as we spotted something in the distance.

We both stopped, and I wasn't sure. Everything looked different. All the trees were taller.

Meg started walking again and reached it first. Surprisingly, the planks were still level after all these years, though they were covered in a film of greenish mold and they were cracked in places where the trees had shifted and grown.

"Yes, this is it." I stepped over a giant root in the ground and my insides stirred with nostalgia. I was only thirteen years old when I hammered those nails. At the time, I'd had no idea where life would take me, or what tragedy would befall the Davenport family.

Meg wandered curiously around the structure, running her fingers lightly along the old wood. "It's sad that you didn't get to finish it."

I nodded and swallowed hard.

Meg craned her neck to look up at the treetops. All I could do was follow her. I was captivated by her beauty, and felt myself falling more and more in love with her with every passing second.

"It would have made a great clubhouse," she said, moving around to the inside of the four trees and looking down at the ground. "Were you planning to build a floor?"

"We never really decided," I said.

She looked down at the ground and back up at the treetops overhead, then held out her hand. "Come and sit down with me."

I joined her. Soon we were lying on our backs, staring up at the sky beyond the branches that swayed in the wind. Meg crossed her legs at the ankles and folded her hands together on her belly. I found myself looking at her, instead of the sky.

"Are you really going to quit your job?" I asked her.

She turned her head to look at me. "I don't know. I'd like to. I think it's time for a change. Change is good." She looked up at the trees again. "I'm imagining that I would like to buy some land on a beach somewhere and build a bunch of cottages, a place where families could go to enjoy themselves and make happy memories."

"That sounds like a great idea," I said, feeling very relaxed.

Meg took a deep breath and let it out. "I just want to do something that makes me feel good. I want to help people make the most of their lives and find the kind of joy we all need to feel. Is that crazy?"

She turned to look at me again and I would have said anything in that moment to make her happy, because nothing else seemed to matter but the rapture I felt in her presence. I wanted to prolong it, hold on to it forever.

"We could start with this place," I said. "I once promised Millicent that we would finish it together. But would *you* finish it with me?"

Meg smiled. "I would *love* to finish this clubhouse with you. But I'll have to insist on a floor, and a good solid roof."

I grinned. "I will bow to your expertise as an accomplished structural engineer."

Meg looked up at the sky again. "What is it about this place that makes me feel so at home? I feel unbelievably happy right now, and I don't know why. I don't think I've ever felt this happy. Not once in my life. I feel so grateful to be alive and to be here with you."

I rolled to the side and leaned on one elbow, stroked her

cheek with the pad of my thumb. "I feel grateful, too. I'm glad I met you, Meg."

She pulled me down for a kiss, and when our lips met, there was no doubt in my mind that I would marry this woman as soon as possible. She was the only one for me. I knew it with every inch of my being.

And one day soon—one day *very* soon—I would tell her why I believed she felt so happy here.

Would she believe it?

As I drew back from the kiss and gazed into her lovely eyes, so full of newfound passion and optimism for the future, I knew somehow, in the depths of my soul, that she would.

Dear Reader,

Thank you for taking the time to read Jack's and Meg's story, which is book 11 in my *Color of Heaven Series*. If you're interested in reading Katelyn's story and learning how she became involved with Jack and Aaron—and how Jack ended up jilted by Katelyn and estranged from his brother—I encourage you to read book 10 in the series: *The Color of Forever*. Up next is a holiday novella entitled *The Color of a Christmas Miracle*. Like all the books in this series, it's based on the theme of real-life magic and miracles that have the power to change people's lives. It's a stand-alone title, and I hope you will check that one out as well.

For more information about the other novels in this series, please read on, or visit my website at www.juliannemaclean.com. While you're there, be sure to sign up for my email newsletter. My subscribers are always first to know about upcoming releases, and I also offer a monthly autographed book giveaway on my website to the members of my newsletter list.

If you read on a Kindle, please visit my author page at Amazon and click the "follow" button to be informed whenever I have a new book out.

You can also follow me on Bookbub if you'd like to know when any of my backlist ebooks go on sale for 99 cents, or if they are offered for free for a very brief time.

I also invite you to follow me on Twitter or Facebook where I chat with readers every day.

Thank you again for reading *The Color of a Promise*, and if you enjoyed the novel, please consider leaving a review at Goodreads or your favorite online retailer to help others discover this series.

As always, happy reading, and lots of love,
Julianne

The COLOR *of* HEAVEN

Book One

A deeply emotional tale about Sophie Duncan, a successful columnist whose world falls apart after her daughter's unexpected illness and her husband's shocking affair. When it seems nothing else could possibly go wrong, her car skids off an icy road and plunges into a frozen lake. There, in the cold dark depths of the water, a profound and extraordinary experience unlocks the surprising secrets from Sophie's past, and teaches her what it means to truly live…and love.

Full of surprising twists and turns and a near-death experience that will leave you breathless, this story is not to be missed.

"A gripping, emotional tale you'll want to read in one sitting."
—*New York Times* bestselling author, Julia London

"Brilliantly poignant mainstream tale."
—4 ½ starred review, *Romantic Times*

Includes Bonus Content: A Bookclub Discussion Guide

The COLOR *of* DESTINY

Book Two

Eighteen years ago a teenage pregnancy changed Kate Worthington's life forever. Faced with many difficult decisions, she chose to follow her heart and embrace an uncertain future with the father of her baby—her devoted first love.

At the same time, in another part of the world, sixteen-year-old Ryan Hamilton makes his own share of mistakes, but learns important lessons along the way. Twenty years later, Kate's and Ryan's paths cross in a way they could never expect, which makes them question the possibility of destiny. Even when all seems hopeless, could it be that everything happens for a reason, and we end up exactly where we are meant to be?

Includes Bonus Content: A Bookclub Discussion Guide

The COLOR *of* HOPE

Book Three

Diana Moore has led a charmed life. She is the daughter of a wealthy senator and lives a glamorous city life, confident that her handsome live-in boyfriend Rick is about to propose. But everything is turned upside down when she learns of a mysterious woman who works nearby—a woman who is her identical mirror image.

Diana is compelled to discover the truth about this woman's identity, but the truth leads her down a path of secrets, betrayals, and shocking discoveries about her past. These discoveries follow her like a shadow.

Then she meets Dr. Jacob Peterson—a brilliant cardiac surgeon with an uncanny ability to heal those who are broken. With his help, Diana embarks upon a journey to restore her belief in the human spirit, and recover a sense of hope—that happiness, and love, may still be within reach for those willing to believe in second chances.

Includes Bonus Content: A Bookclub Discussion Guide

The COLOR *of* A DREAM

Book Four

Nadia Carmichael has had a lifelong run of bad luck. It begins on the day she is born, when she is separated from her identical twin sister and put up for adoption. Twenty-seven years later, not long after she is finally reunited with her twin and is expecting her first child, Nadia falls victim to a mysterious virus and requires a heart transplant.

Now recovering from the surgery with a new heart, Nadia is haunted by a recurring dream that sets her on a path to discover the identity of her donor. Her efforts are thwarted, however, when the father of her baby returns to sue for custody of their child. It's not until Nadia learns of his estranged brother Jesse that she begins to explore the true nature of her dreams, and discover what her new heart truly needs and desires…

The COLOR *of* A MEMORY

Book Five

Audrey Fitzgerald believed she was married to the perfect man—a heroic firefighter who saved lives, even beyond his own death. But a year later she meets a mysterious woman who has some unexplained connection to her husband…

Soon Audrey discovers that her husband was keeping secrets and she is compelled to dig into his past. Little does she know…this journey of self-discovery will lead her down a path to a new and different future—a future she never could have imagined.

The COLOR *of* LOVE

Book Six

Carla Matthews is a single mother struggling to make ends meet and give her daughter Kaleigh a decent upbringing. When Kaleigh's absent father Seth—a famous alpine climber who never wanted to be tied down—begs for a second chance at fatherhood, Carla is hesitant because she doesn't want to pin her hopes on a man who is always seeking another mountain to scale. A man who was never willing to stay put in one place and raise a family.

But when Seth's plane goes missing after a crash landing in the harsh Canadian wilderness, Carla must wait for news… Is he dead or alive? Will the wreckage ever be found?

One year later, after having given up all hope, Carla receives a phone call that shocks her to her core. A man has been found, half-dead, floating on an iceberg in the North Atlantic, uttering her name. Is this Seth? And is it possible that he will come home to her and Kaleigh at last, and be the man she always dreamed he would be?

Includes Bonus Content: A Bookclub Discussion Guide

The COLOR *of* THE SEASON

Book Seven

From *USA Today* bestselling author Julianne MacLean comes the next installment in her popular Color of Heaven series—a gripping, emotional tale about real life magic that touches us all during the holiday season…

Boston cop, Josh Wallace, is having the worst day of his life. First, he's dumped by the woman he was about to propose to, then everything goes downhill from there when he is shot in the line of duty. While recovering in the hospital, he can't seem to forget the woman he wanted to marry, nor can he make sense of the vivid images that flashed before his eyes when he was wounded on the job. Soon, everything he once believed about his life begins to shift when he meets Leah James, an enigmatic resident doctor who somehow holds the key to both his past and his future…

The COLOR of JOY

Book Eight

After rushing to the hospital for the birth of their third child, Riley and Lois James anticipate one of the most joyful days of their lives. But things take a dark turn when their newborn daughter vanishes from the hospital. Is this payback for something in Riley's troubled past? Or is it something even more mysterious?

As the search intensifies and the police close in, strange and unbelievable clues about the whereabouts of the newborn begin to emerge, and Riley soon finds himself at the center of a surprising turn of events that will challenge everything he once believed about life, love, and the existence of miracles.

The COLOR of TIME

Book Nine

They say it's impossible to change the past...

Since her magical summer romance at the age of sixteen, Sylvie Nichols has never been able to forget her first love.

Years later, when she returns to the seaside town where she lost her heart to Ethan Foster, she is determined to lay the past to rest once and for all. But letting go becomes a challenge when Sylvie finds herself transported back to that long ago summer of love...and the turbulent events that followed. Soon, past and present begin to collide in strange and mystifying ways, and Sylvie can't help but wonder if a true belief in miracles is powerful enough to change both her past and her future....

The COLOR of FOREVER

Book Ten

Recently divorced television reporter Katelyn Roberts has stopped believing in relationships that last forever, until a near-death experience during a cycling accident changes everything. When she miraculously survives unscathed, a long-buried mystery leads her to the quaint, seaside town of Cape Elizabeth, Maine.

There, on the rugged, windswept coast of the Atlantic, she finds herself caught up in the secrets of a historic inn that somehow calls to her from the past. Is it possible that the key to her true destiny lies beneath all that she knows, as she explores the grand mansion and property? Or that the great love she's always dreamed of is hidden in the alcoves of its past?

"I never know what to say about a Julianne MacLean book, except to say YOU HAVE TO READ IT."
— *AllRomanceReader.ca*

Coming in October 2016

The COLOR
of a
CHRISTMAS
MIRACLE

"It makes the reader think about what could have been, and loves past, and makes you wonder if you are leading the life you're meant to be leading. Thought-provoking, emotionally-intense and riveting, Ms. MacLean delivers another 5-star romance in The Color of Forever."

—Nancy at Goodreads

"Wow! The Color of Heaven was intriguing, emotional, heartbreaking, inspiring, breathtaking, and touched me very profoundly. You will not be able to put it down but I encourage you to absorb the depth of the characters and their journeys. Thank you!!"

—Amazon reviewer

"Spell Binding! My first read by Julianne…wow, I am hooked! I couldn't stop reading this intriguing story. Look forward to the next one."

—Iris at Amazon

"Emotionally moving! There are many twists, some predictable, some not. Heartfelt!"

—GEA at Amazon

"Loved it!"   —Christa at Amazon

"Fabulous read. I thoroughly enjoyed this book. Well written. Lots of interesting subjects covered. Characters lovely and rich. A worthwhile read! Looking forward to sampling the next book in the series."

—Sandra at Amazon

"Heavenly book!"   —Bobbi at Amazon

Praise for Julianne MacLean's Historical Romances

"MacLean's compelling writing turns this simple, classic love story into a richly emotional romance, and by combining engaging characters with a unique, vividly detailed setting, she has created an exceptional tale for readers who hunger for something a bit different in their historical romances."

—*BOOKLIST*

"You can always count on Julianne MacLean to deliver ravishing romance that will keep you turning pages until the wee hours of the morning."

—Teresa Medeiros

"Julianne MacLean's writing is smart, thrilling, and sizzles with sensuality."

—Elizabeth Hoyt

"Scottish romance at its finest, with characters to cheer for, a lush love story, and rousing adventure. I was captivated from the very first page. When it comes to exciting Highland romance, Julianne MacLean delivers."

—Laura Lee Guhrke

"She is just an all-around wonderful writer, and I look forward to reading everything she writes."

—*Romance Junkies*

About the Author

Julianne MacLean is a *USA Today* bestselling author of many historical romances, including The Highlander Series with St. Martin's Press and her popular American Heiress Series with Avon/Harper Collins. She also writes contemporary mainstream fiction, and The Color of Heaven was a *USA Today* bestseller. She is a three-time RITA finalist, and has won numerous awards, including the Booksellers' Best Award, the Book Buyer's Best Award, and a Reviewers' Choice Award from Romantic Times for Best Regency Historical of 2005. She lives in Nova Scotia with her husband and daughter, and is a dedicated member of Romance Writers of Atlantic Canada. Please visit Julianne's website for more information and to subscribe to her mailing list to stay informed about upcoming releases.

www.juliannemaclean.com

OTHER BOOKS BY
JULIANNE MACLEAN

The American Heiress Series
To Marry the Duke
An Affair Most Wicked
My Own Private Hero
Love According to Lily
Portrait of a Lover
Surrender to a Scoundrel

The Pembroke Palace Series
In My Wildest Fantasies
The Mistress Diaries
When a Stranger Loves Me
Married By Midnight
A Kiss Before the Wedding – A Pembroke Palace Short Story
Seduced at Sunset

The Highlander Trilogy
The Rebel – A Highland Short Story
Captured by the Highlander
Claimed by the Highlander
Seduced by the Highlander
Return of the Highlander
Taken by the Highlander

The Royal Trilogy

Be My Prince
Princess in Love
The Prince's Bride

Dodge City Brides Trilogy

Mail Order Prairie Bride
Tempting the Marshal
Taken by the Cowboy – a Time Travel Romance

Colonial Romance

Adam's Promise

Contemporary Fiction

The Color of Heaven
The Color of Destiny
The Color of Hope
The Color of a Dream
The Color of a Memory
The Color of Love
The Color of the Season
The Color of Joy
The Color of Time
The Color of Forever
The Color of a Promise
The Color of a Christmas Miracle